Designs on Love

a novella by

Myra Johnson

ISBN: 1537720953
ISBN-13: 978-1537720951

Cover photography by
Rodian Kutsaev, unsplash.com/@frostroomhead
Annie Spratt, unsplash.com/@fableandfolk

Dedication

With gratitude to Kassie Collins
for providing the name for my heroine,
Vera Mae Beasley, named for Kassie's late mother.
While the real Vera Mae was also from Bryan, Texas,
and enjoyed sewing clothes for her daughters,
the rest of this story is strictly from my imagination.

Designs on Love

CHAPTER ONE

FRIDAY, SEPTEMBER 20, 1867
Philadelphia, Pennsylvania

"It's perfect, simply perfect!" Vera Mae Beasley twirled in front of the cheval mirror in her aunt's boudoir. The mauve ball gown with bell-shaped overskirt and ivory lace ruffles had turned out exactly as she'd envisioned.

Aunt Cassandra clapped her hands. "My dear, you'll be the envy of every young lady at the dance."

There was only one person Vera hoped to impress: renowned Paris fashion designer Madame Solange Fortier. If Vera could obtain an apprenticeship at Madame Fortier's exclusive Philadelphia dress shop, she would be well on her way to the future she'd dreamed of ever since her mother first taught her to sew a stitch.

Thoughts of her mother rekindled the homesickness plaguing Vera. Two years ago, her parents, mercantile owners in Millican, Texas, had sent her to Philadelphia to live with her aunt and uncle, Cassandra and Reginald Beasley. After the war ended, Papa thought the North a safer, more civilized setting for a young lady to continue her education and perhaps meet a respectable gentleman to marry.

Marriage? It was the last thing on Vera's mind. She arranged a dark brown ringlet across her shoulder, then tugged at the ivory bow on her bustle. "Have I used too much lace, Aunt Cassie?"

"Absolutely not. It's—" A knock sounded on the outer door, and Cassandra rose to answer. "Yes, Maddie?"

"A telegram, ma'am." The maid curtsied as she handed Cassandra an envelope.

Dismissing Maddie with a nod, Cassandra slid the telegram from the envelope. As she read silently, her expression turned grim. She pressed one fist to her lips and sank into the nearest chair. "Oh, no. Dear God, no!"

"Aunt Cassie?" Vera gathered up her skirts and rushed over. "What is it?"

Cassandra's lower lip trembled. She reached for Vera's hand. "You'd best sit down, my dear."

Throat clenching, Vera dropped to the chair across from her aunt. "Please, tell me what it says."

"Your mother—" Cassandra choked on a sob.

Vera snatched the telegram from her aunt's hand and read it for herself:

Yellow fever outbreak. Lorna died 17 Sept, Martin 2 days later. Many more sick. Town in chaos. Under no circumstances is Vera to come home.

"Mama and my brother—*dead*?" Crushing the flimsy paper against her bosom, Vera gasped for breath. While her heart struggled to accept the devastating news, her brain rushed ahead to more practical matters. She shoved to her feet. "I'll pack my trunks at once. Perhaps there's a train yet leaving this afternoon."

"Vera, you can't." Cassandra stood and clutched Vera's arms. "Your father forbade it. It's too dangerous."

"But he's all alone now. He might already be sick himself." Vera glanced anxiously toward the door.

"Be sensible, child. What good will you be to your father if you catch this dreadful disease yourself? Best to wait and pray God will bring an end to the epidemic soon."

"But who will take care of Papa? Who will manage the mercantile?"

Aunt Cassandra slowly shook her head. "If things are as dire as this telegram suggests, there is nothing you could do. If you go home now, just imagine how your father will worry over you. He'll need you even more once the worst is past."

Vera couldn't deny the wisdom of her aunt's words, but how could she bear the agony of waiting, of wondering whether she'd have any family left to go home to?

Tuesday, October 8, 1867

A ranch southwest of Bryan, Texas

Jacob Collins eased back on the reins, drawing the wagon to a halt next to Georgia Richardson's whitewashed porch. "Back with the supplies, ma'am," he called through the open kitchen door.

The gray-haired widow appeared with a dishtowel draped over her shoulder. Grinning, she marched down the porch steps. "Just in time. I'll need the flour for tonight's biscuits. Hope you're hungry, 'cause I made a big pot of stew."

"Starved." Jacob jumped down from the wagon seat and started unloading the supplies.

Hefting one of the smaller crates, Miz Georgia, as she liked to be called, followed him into the kitchen. Her tone grew serious. "What's the word in town?"

Jacob's mouth flattened. He set a bag of dried beans on a pantry shelf. "Yellow fever's still running rampant, even worse toward the coast. Houston and Galveston are getting hit hard."

"Then it's good we're this far inland, and not too close to town." Miz Georgia opened the flour sack and measured out a cupful. "You're being careful, aren't you? Not breathing that foul air or exposing yourself to anyone who's sick?"

"Doesn't seem to matter much. Nobody knows for sure how the disease is spread." Jacob reached into a crate for the newspaper he'd brought from town and laid it on the counter next to the flour sack. "Latest deaths are on page three if you want to look."

She frowned. "Not sure I do."

Jacob had recognized more than a few names on the list—some in Bryan and even more down in Millican, where Jacob had grown up. He was saddened to see Albert Beasley's name and wondered if Vera Mae had received word about her father's passing. With her mother and brother already dead and buried, she must be heartbroken. Jacob hoped her Philadelphia relatives were keeping her there, far, far away from the deadly sickness ravaging coastal Texas. If anything happened to Vera . . .

Miz Georgia floured her rolling pin. "Got time to fetch more wood for the cook stove?"

"Sure thing." Jacob set the last of the groceries in the pantry. "Then I'd better see if Esteban and Hector rounded up those strays."

"Supper'll be on the table by the time you get back. Tell the boys to get a move on."

Jacob set his hat firmly on his head and started out the door. He was mighty grateful to have this job as ranch foreman, and for more reasons than the paycheck. He'd come home from the war to find his own widowed mother had passed away. With no family left and needing work, he'd asked around first in Millican and then in Bryan. Finally, someone sent him out to Georgia Richardson's place. The kindhearted woman had offered him not just gainful employment but real friendship, all the while putting meat on his bones with her delicious home cooking.

The aroma of Miz Georgia's savory beef stew followed Jacob all the way to the barn. When he spied Esteban's buckskin and Hector's sorrel munching hay in their stalls, he figured the boys must be back from checking on the crew working the south pasture. With any luck, they'd found the stray yearlings that had wandered off in the night. Miz Georgia's cattle herd might be small, but the stock was of the finest quality, generating enough income to keep the ranch profitable.

Which was a real good thing for Jacob and the hired hands.

And someday, if things turned out like Jacob hoped, Georgia Richardson's ranch would be his.

CHAPTER TWO

VERA STOOD BEFORE her dressing table as Maddie buttoned up the plain black mourning dress. With red-rimmed eyes and sunken cheeks, she could barely stand to look at herself in the mirror. There'd been too many tears shed over the past month.

The letter from Ephraim Polk, owner of a competing mercantile in Millican, had arrived three days ago. He'd made what seemed a fair offer to buy the Beasleys' building and remaining inventory, but the thought of signing away the shop her parents had poured their lives into tore at Vera's conscience.

No, as the only living heir, she must return home and salvage what she could of the family business. She'd helped in the store from the time she could add figures and read product labels. Somehow she would keep Beasley Mercantile going. It was the best way she knew to honor her family's memory.

Aunt Cassandra tiptoed into the room. "It's time, dear. Your trunks are in the carriage, and your uncle is ready to take you to the train."

Shoulders squared, Vera brushed away a trace of wetness from her face before reaching for her reticule. At the look of worry furrowing her aunt's brow, she enfolded her in a warm embrace. "Don't worry. I'll take every care, I promise."

Cassandra held on as if she'd never let go. "I do wish you'd wait another few weeks. Let the epidemic run its course."

"I've waited long enough already. I didn't even get a chance to tell my family a final good-bye, and now—" Vera swallowed the lump in her throat. "And now the mercantile is my responsibility." With a final squeeze, she broke free.

A tearful good-bye to her aunt before stepping into the carriage, another sad farewell as Uncle Reggie saw her onto the train, and soon Vera watched the Pennsylvania landscape disappear behind her.

Four days later and utterly overwhelmed by emotion and exhaustion, Vera sat at her father's desk, head in her hands. After paging through ledgers and riffling through filing cabinets, she could clearly see the business was failing—had been since long before the yellow fever epidemic took hold. In fact, the whole town had been in a decline since the Houston and Texas Central Railway had moved its terminus from Millican to Bryan.

Dear God, how would she ever pay off all the debts Papa had left behind, much less get the store operational again?

The creak of boards startled her. She raised her head to see Ephraim Polk step into the office.

"Miss Beasley," he said, removing his bowler. "I heard you'd arrived in town. May I personally offer my deepest condolences." He cleared his throat. "I trust you received my letter?"

"I did." Vera rose stiffly. "However, I am not yet prepared to make any decisions regarding the disposition of Beasley

Mercantile."

The balding man crossed slowly in front of the desk, two fingers trailing through the dust along the edge. He paused with a grimace to examine his fingertips, then wiped them with his handkerchief. "Surely you can see there's no hope here. My own Millican store is struggling, which is why I opened a branch in Bryan. I've offered you a fair price for your father's assets, including the goodwill he earned as a shopkeeper. I'd advise you to unburden yourself and return posthaste to the *much* more comfortable life you have enjoyed in Philadelphia."

"I'm grateful for your concern, Mr. Polk, and I promise to give your offer serious consideration." Vera's thoughts went to the ledger entries she'd just reviewed. Her stomach twisted with the nagging sense that even if she accepted Ephraim Polk's offer, there still wouldn't be enough to erase the debt her father had accrued.

"Very well. But don't wait too long, or what's left of your inventory won't be worth selling."

Hoping to hurry him on his way, she took her seat and folded her hands atop the ledger. "Good day, Mr. Polk. I'll be in touch."

Jacob had no good reason to ride over to Millican. Except one. In church last Sunday, he'd overheard a couple of former Millicanites talking about the Beasley Mercantile, and wasn't it a shame about poor Vera Mae coming home to permanently close the store.

He'd barged in on their conversation. "Vera's coming home? When?"

"Why, sometime this week," one of the old biddies replied. "I heard it from Iola Jackson, who knows Matilda Horne, who got it direct from—"

Jacob didn't care how far along the grapevine the news had traveled. He only cared about seeing Vera Mae again. Ranch work had kept him too busy all week to break away, so by Saturday he was antsier than a bronc with a burr under the saddle. After making sure Esteban and Hector could handle things at the ranch, he made excuses to Miz Georgia and aimed his horse toward Millican.

Riding along deserted streets past empty storefronts, Jacob felt a tug in his chest. If people kept moving out, Millican would soon be little more than a ghost town.

It was nearing noon when he reined his horse to a halt in front of Beasley Mercantile. The shades were drawn, but the front door stood ajar. With his horse secured to the hitching post, he sidled up the steps. As he peered into the dark interior, a stale odor of dust and mildew made him wrinkle his nose. "Hello?" he called. "Anybody here?"

Rustling sounds came from the rear office. Then a soft sniffle, and a woman's shaky voice replied, "Yes, who is it?"

Vera Mae. Jacob's long strides carried him through the store and into the back hallway. Before he made it through the office door, a slim female figure crashed against him. He did the only thing he could—throw his arms around her and hold on tight.

"Oh. Oh!" Gasping, Vera pressed her hands against Jacob's chest. She tipped her head, eyes wide as dinner plates. "Jacob? *Jacob Collins?*"

"In the flesh." Blessed be, if she wasn't even prettier than the last time he'd seen her. Softer and rounder, too, in all the right places. Then, realizing the drift of his thoughts, he decided he might ought to remove his arms from around her waist and put a few inches between them.

Stepping back, Vera smoothed her skirt with one hand and her silky brown curls with the other. Even in black, she looked like a picture from one of those fashion catalogues she always had her nose buried in. "Goodness, Jacob, what a surprise! I expected you'd be long gone from Millican by now."

"Thought about it, especially coming home from the war to find my folks dead and buried." He winced, realizing Vera still grieved the loss of her own family. "But Texas is my home and I've still got friends here, so I found work at a ranch outside Bryan."

"That's wonderful." She looked relieved, somehow. And then a tear escaped. "I was terrified I'd come home to find everyone I cared about had either died or moved on."

She cared about him? Probably not the way he'd always hoped she would, but his heart did a little flip all the same. Jacob yanked off his dusty hat and rolled the brim with nervous hands. "I'm real sorry about your family, Vera Mae."

"Thank you." She dabbed at the corners of her eyes with a lacy white handkerchief. "I wanted to come home sooner, but my aunt and uncle wouldn't allow it."

"They were wise to keep you away. We're all hoping the worst has passed, but it's been bad, real bad."

"I thought nothing could be worse than getting those telegrams about my parents and brother, but coming home to the empty store—" Stifling a sob with her fist, Vera gazed past Jacob toward the front doors. "It's a thousand times harder than I ever imagined."

Jacob could no more have stopped himself from taking her in his arms again than he could have grown another head. Besides, she smelled like freshly cut lilacs and fit so perfectly beneath his chin. "I've got you, Vera Mae. It'll be all right."

It was quite unseemly to take such comfort in a man's embrace. Especially unchaperoned in a deserted building. As soon as Vera felt a semblance of control returning, she patted Jacob's chest and gently pushed away.

My, how he'd filled out, his muscled arms solid as oak. His face had lost some of its boyish roundness, no doubt in part from the rigors of war. Poor Jacob had been a victim of the Confederate Conscription Act and forced to fight for the South. Praise God he'd returned alive.

"So you're a ranch hand," Vera said, arms folded against her ribcage.

"A ranch foreman, actually." More than a little pride tinged Jacob's tone. "I work for Georgia Richardson."

"I've heard of the Richardsons. In fact, I'm certain I've seen the name in my father's account books." Vera nodded toward the office behind her, and her lungs deflated at the reminder of all those debts. She trudged around the desk and sank into the chair with a groan.

Jacob stood across from her. "That bad, huh?" He motioned toward the ledgers and invoices spread across the desk. "How long have you been at this?"

"Three days." She gave a helpless shrug. "My father's letters over the past year never gave any indication of how poor business had been. I'm afraid I'll have no choice but to accept Ephraim Polk's offer to buy us out."

"Is that what you want to do?" Jacob asked softly.

Vera's chin shot up. "My parents poured their whole lives into the mercantile." A catch in her throat, she glanced away. "We had such grand plans."

Pulling a chair closer, Jacob sat on the edge, his mouth slanted in a sympathetic frown. "I'm so sorry, Vera Mae. No one could have predicted what happened to Millican."

She slammed a ledger shut, sending a puff of dust into the air. "It's pointless postponing the inevitable. I should tell Ephraim I'm ready to sell."

Jacob nodded grimly. They sat in silence for several moments before he asked, "What will you do, then? Go back to Philly?"

"Not right away. Somehow, I'll have to figure out how to pay off the remaining debt."

"But if you sell the store, what's left?"

"Just our house, the furniture—" More tears threatened. Vera pressed her handkerchief to her lips. "Oh, Jacob, when I have so many good memories here, how can I part with it all?"

"You don't need *things* to keep your family's memories alive in your heart." Jacob's voice was firm but kind. "If the war taught me anything, it's that people are way more important than possessions."

"I know you're right." Stiffening her spine, Vera push

feet. "I must be brave about this. Papa would expect no less. I'll just . . ."

A wave of dizziness buckled her knees. She saw the corner of the desk rushing toward her face before she blessedly blacked out. Her last conscious thought was that hitting the desk should have hurt much worse than it did.

CHAPTER THREE

"EASY THERE!" THREE quick strides brought Jacob to Vera's side. He threw his arms around her an instant before she would have knocked herself silly on the edge of the desk. Easing her limp body into the chair, he felt her cheeks and forehead. She was clammy and pale, but not in a feverish kind of way, thank the Lord.

Vera lifted her head and glanced around dazedly. "Oh, my. How embarrassing."

Weak with relief, Jacob bent to retrieve his hat, which he'd dropped in his mad rush to rescue Vera. "You scared me somethin' awful. Are you sure you're okay?"

"Fatigue must be catching up with me." Vera massaged her temple. "I haven't slept much since leaving Philadelphia."

On a nearby filing cabinet, Jacob spied a plate containing most of a dried-out sandwich. "Or eaten much either, is my guess. You've got to take better care of yourself."

"I know, and I will." She looked about ready to pass out again. "After I—"

"No, now. You're coming with me."

Jacob didn't give Vera a chance to argue. Lifting her to her feet, he propelled her through the store. He let her sit on a bench out front long enough for him to lock up, then steered her over to his waiting horse and prepared to boost her into the saddle.

By then, she'd come to her senses enough to put up a fuss. "Jacob Collins, what on earth are you doing?"

"Taking care of you. What's it look like?"

Vera huffed and whirled around. "It *looks* like you're enjoying the view of my bustle a teensy bit too much."

The horse whinnied and sidestepped, and Jacob reached out a calming hand. "Easy, now, Curly."

"Don't you talk to me like—" Vera's brows shot up. She looked from Jacob to the mare and back again. "You named your *horse* Curly?"

Gulping, Jacob forced a grin. "See, her forelock has this little kink in it, kind of like . . . well . . ." His gaze slid to the soft brown curls gracing Vera's shoulder.

"You gave your horse the nickname you always called me when we were kids? Honestly, Jacob, I don't know whether to be flattered or offended."

"Your choice," he said, trying to regain the upper hand in this conversation. "While you figure it out, I'd appreciate it if you'd allow me to set you in the saddle so I can take you somewhere for a decent meal." Preferably up the road a ways where there was less chance of yellow fever catching up with them. He didn't care one bit for the idea of Vera hanging around Millican any longer than necessary.

Starting to look a little shaky again, Vera rested a hand at her waist. "I guess I should try to eat. I just haven't had much appetite."

"Understandable." Jacob glanced up the street. "Tell you what. I'll run in the cafe over yonder and order us some food. Then we can go to your house—"

"No, please. I can't." Vera clutched his sleeve, a desperate look twisting her features.

Jacob studied her. "You haven't been home at all, have you?"

She shook her head. "It was hard enough coming back to the store, sitting at my father's desk. I couldn't bring myself to step inside our empty house."

"Where have you been staying?"

Her gaze slid toward the mercantile.

"The whole time you've been back? Aw, Vera." He tucked her beneath his chin. "That settles it. Once we get you something to eat, I'm taking you to the ranch. Miz Georgia's got an extra room, and I know she'd be pleased to give you a place to rest while you figure things out."

Besides, at the ranch, Jacob would be right there to keep an eye on her.

Except his intentions went way beyond seeing to Vera's welfare. Maybe God was smiling on him after all, because for half his young life, Jacob Collins had but one dream: to make Vera Mae Beasley his wife.

Vera watched from the window of Georgia Richardson's upstairs guest room as Jacob led Curly—*Curly!*—into the barn. If she had to have a horse as her namesake, at least this horse was both gentle and smart. A light touch on the reins or subtle pressure with his knee was all Jacob needed. He claimed Curly was the best cutting horse for miles around and counted himself blessed to own her.

When Mrs. Richardson tapped on the open bedroom door, Vera turned with a grateful smile. “How can I ever thank you for your kindness?”

“Honey, don’t you even worry about it.” The white-haired woman looked too dainty to be a rancher, but Vera detected an air of strength and determination, qualities Vera would need in abundance to make it through the weeks to come. Mrs. Richardson laid clean folded towels at the foot of the bed. “Make yourself right at home, you hear? Jacob sent Hector back to Millican with the buckboard to pick up your trunks. Supper will be on the table at six-thirty sharp, but if you’re too tired to come down, I’ll bring you a tray.”

“I wouldn’t think of troubling you further, Mrs. Richardson. As soon as I freshen up, I’ll come downstairs and help.”

“Only if you feel up to it. And call me Miz Georgia. Everyone else does.” With a wink, the woman stepped through the door and pulled it closed.

First Jacob and now Miz Georgia—Vera hadn’t felt this loved and cared for since leaving Aunt Cassie behind in Philadelphia.

And Miz Georgia’s featherbed was so, so comfortable. Vera thought she’d lie down for just a moment or two, only to wake with a start at the sound of boisterous male voices coming from the kitchen. A glance at the watch pinned to her bodice told her it was already well past six o'clock. She hurried to splash cool water on her face and run a brush through her hair.

At the foot of the stairs, Vera paused and peered around the corner into the kitchen. Jacob and two other men, all of them looking freshly scrubbed and their wet hair slicked back, followed Miz Georgia's orders as she got supper on the table.

When Jacob noticed her standing in the doorway, his grin widened. He handed the serving bowl he carried to one of the other men and then offered Vera his arm. "Hector's back with your things. Looks like you had a nice rest."

"I did, and it was lovely." She let Jacob escort her to the table, where he pulled out a chair for her. "Thank you." Adjusting her skirt, she looked up at him meaningfully. "Thank you for everything."

A delicious meal, a good night's sleep, and Vera awoke with more energy than she'd had in days. Miz Georgia had told her they'd all be going to church in Bryan on Sunday morning and Vera was welcome to come along if she felt up to it. She decided she did. Since so many former Millican residents had moved to Bryan, she might even see some old friends.

And she could certainly use all the support she could get.

"My, don't you look pretty," Miz Georgia remarked when Vera came downstairs. "I know you're in mourning, but even all in black, your dress is quite becoming."

With a sad smile, Vera smoothed the sash at her waist. "After getting word about my family, and with my aunt and uncle refusing to let me come home a day sooner, I had plenty of time to sew mourning gowns."

Surprise lit Miz Georgia's eyes. "You made this yourself? Dearie me, what a gift you have! Why, I may need to engage your services to freshen up my wardrobe."

"If time permits, I'd love to." Vera accepted the plate of scrambled eggs and biscuits Miz Georgia handed her and carried it to the table. "My parents sent me to Philadelphia to further my education and study fashion design. It's been a dream of mine since I was a little girl. But now . . ." She stared at the plate of food, a fresh wave of grief stealing her appetite.

"I expect your folks wouldn't be happy about you giving up on your dreams." Miz Georgia patted her shoulder. "You'll find your way again. Your heart just needs some space to heal."

Vera doubted she'd ever heal from the loss of her family. But Miz Georgia was right. She shouldn't waste the opportunities her parents had worked so hard to give her.

She coaxed down enough breakfast to keep her stomach from making noises in church. Jacob brought the buckboard around, and with Vera sandwiched between him and Miz Georgia on the seat, and the two ranch hands in back, they set off for Bryan. Brushing elbows, hips, and knees with Jacob, Vera was glad they weren't alone in the wagon. At least this wasn't as awkward as the ride out from Millican yesterday. Mounted behind her on Curly's back, Jacob had held her tightly against his chest, while his warm breath tickled her ear.

A tiny chuckle worked its way up her throat. Poking her elbow hard into Jacob's side, she slanted him an accusing smirk. "I still can't believe you named your horse Curly."

His only reply was a smug smile and a lift of his brow.

The worship service was like balm to Vera's spirit. Afterward, she welcomed the many greetings from old friends who'd since moved to Bryan. They extended their sympathies and commiserated with her over her hometown's decline.

"But Bryan's bustling, let me tell you," Vera's former schoolteacher told her. "Now that Bryan's the county seat and the railroad extends this far, why, this town will just grow and grow."

Miz Georgia suggested lunch at a hotel restaurant downtown, and Vera could hardly believe how Bryan had grown since the last time she'd been here. When they passed Polk's General Store, a two-story building with broad display windows filled with merchandise, Vera had to look away. Poor Papa, to struggle as he did while his competitor flourished.

When they arrived at the restaurant, Hector and Esteban excused themselves to meet friends at a cafe down the street. Jacob showed Vera and Miz Georgia to a quiet table near the window. They'd barely sat down when Ephraim Polk and his wife approached their table.

"Hello, Miss Beasley." Ephraim cast her a benevolent smile. "I see you're already enjoying Bryan's hospitality. May I assume this means you're giving serious thought to my offer?"

"I told you I would," Vera answered coolly. "But I cannot make any decisions regarding my family's interests until I've weighed every option."

"I would expect nothing less." With a nod to his wife, Ephraim sent her on to their table, then pulled out an empty chair and sat at Vera's left. At her lifted brow, he said, "Forgive the intrusion on your Sunday dinner, but I do understand the difficult situation you find yourself in . . . financially speaking, that is."

"Mr. Polk," Jacob interrupted, "this *is* an intrusion, and I'll thank you to discuss business matters with Miss Beasley at a more appropriate time."

Hands raised, Ephraim stood. "My apologies. Miss Beasley, if we could talk sometime in the next day or two, I have a proposition to present—something I believe would be equally beneficial for both of us."

Vera eyed him warily. "As you can imagine, I have quite a lot to attend to. I'm not sure what the next few days will bring."

"Of course. Should you find the time, I'll be at the Bryan store during business hours most of this week." With a polite dip of his chin, Ephraim strode away.

Jacob harrumphed. "I can just imagine what kind of *proposition* that snake oil salesman has on his mind."

"Now, Jacob," Miz Georgia chided, "Ephraim may sometimes put profit before people, but he's a respectable businessman."

Swallowing a sip of water, Vera watched as Ephraim joined his wife and a young couple across the dining room. If she wasn't mistaken, the girl was Ephraim's only daughter, Nancy, who'd been two grades ahead of Vera in school. If loving glances meant anything, the man with Nancy must be her beau. When they leaned close for a quick kiss, Vera looked away.

Over a dinner of fried chicken, mashed potatoes, and creamed peas, Vera pondered what Ephraim's proposition might be. If there was any chance it might alleviate her late parents' massive load of debt, she owed it to herself to find out more.

CHAPTER FOUR

"I'M TELLING YOU, Vera Mae, there's no earthly reason for you to go back to the mercantile." Jacob knew he was acting like a spoiled kid stomping his foot like he did, but two more cases of yellow fever had been reported in Millican, and he wasn't about to let Vera risk her health—maybe even her life—by spending any more time there than necessary.

With a gloved hand, Vera tucked aside the veil of black mesh draping her bonnet. "If a germ or miasma or whatever is causing this disease can find its way through all these clothes, it's welcome to have at me."

Jacob suppressed a shudder. "Don't say such things."

"Sorry, it's just my frustration talking." She lightly touched his arm. "But I still have so much to sort through at the store. Before I can make a deal with Ephraim Polk, I need to understand exactly what I'm faced with."

Even through her leather riding glove, the warmth of her hand soaked right through his shirtsleeve. It took all his willpower to focus on the words he needed to say. "Then let me go fetch what you need and bring it back here. I'll leave in the buckboard right now. I can be back by mid-afternoon."

She tipped her head, the bonnet brim hiding her features. Her shoulders rose and fell in a reluctant sigh. "I admit, I don't look forward to spending endless hours alone in an empty building." When she glanced up, a tentative smile curled her lips. "Let's go over together. I'll gather the records I need—you wouldn't know anyway—and we'll box them up so I can work on them here."

Drawing a hand across his jaw, Jacob decided it was a fair compromise. "I'll hitch up the wagon."

"And I'll drive." With a strut in her step, Vera marched to the corral. She chose one of the halters hanging on the gate. "Which horses are we taking?"

"Now hold on." Jacob jogged to catch up. "How long has it been since you wrangled a horse? Not since you left for Philly, I'm guessing."

"Maybe not, but there was a time not so long ago that I could outride you." She reached for the gate latch.

Jacob's hand clamped down on hers. "Not since you were a kid in pigtails." So close he could hear the startled flutter in her breath, he fought to keep his own pulse from racing. He suddenly wanted to kiss her so badly, it hurt.

"Jacob . . . the horses . . ." Her voice barely a whisper, she broke eye contact.

A lump the size of one of Miz Georgia's plump biscuits rose in Jacob's throat. He fumbled for the latch and swung the gate open. "You can get the sorrel over yonder with the white blaze. Name's Charlie. I'll get Duke here and meet you at the buckboard."

Soon the horses were hitched to the wagon, and as Jacob should have expected, Vera insisted on taking the reins. She clearly hadn't forgotten much during her time out east. The horses took to her right away, and she had a light but steady hand with them. Once assured she needed no help from him, he sat back and enjoyed the ride.

Arriving in Millican, Vera wasted no time in gathering the ledgers and files she wanted. Jacob found a couple of empty crates and loaded everything into the buckboard. On the way back to the ranch, they stopped by a stream for a picnic lunch.

The late-October day was warm, so Vera peeled off her bonnet and shook out her curls. Jacob had to hide his disappointment when she gathered her hair in a twist and pinned it in a loose bun. Did she have any idea what he felt for her—how much he'd cared for her since he'd figured out girls were meant for other things than torturing with frogs down their backs or swiping their spelling books?

If so, she gave no sign. Vera's first love, apart from her family, had been the mercantile, especially the dry goods section. When Jacob would come by to fill his mother's grocery list, he'd often find Vera measuring out fabric and talking lace and trim with one of her father's customers. She'd always had an eye for style and color, and now it saddened Jacob to see her swathed in shades of black and gray. She'd lost so much, yet she remained strong and determined.

Determined to return to Philly, no doubt. If Jacob had any hope of winning her heart, he needed to make it happen soon.

It was Wednesday before Vera felt she'd made enough headway with the mercantile accounts to accurately assess where things stood. After Mama and Martin had taken ill, her father's record keeping became sporadic. At the time of their deaths it had ceased entirely, with orders and invoices stuffed haphazardly into drawers and filing cabinets. Then Papa took ill and nothing had been done since. Vera had to bring weeks of ledger entries up to date.

With each entry the debts climbed higher. Her original rough estimate now seemed ridiculously optimistic.

It was time to speak with Ephraim Polk.

"I need to ride into town," she told Miz Georgia as she moved a crate of files off the dining table.

Stirring a pot of bean soup on the stove, Miz Georgia nodded. "Pick me up some baking powder and a can of peaches, if you don't mind."

"Glad to." Vera didn't have to explain her reasons for the trip. Miz Georgia had sat with her often over the past few days and listened to her mounting worry over the state of the mercantile accounts.

Jacob and the ranch hands were out with the cattle, so Miz Georgia left her soup long enough to point out Dusty, a gentle buckskin mare, and show Vera which saddle and bridle to use. Clad in a dark gray jacket and black riding skirt, Vera headed toward Bryan.

In town, she found her way to Polk's General Store. Averting her eyes from the gaudy window displays, she stepped inside.

A towheaded young clerk scurried over. "How can I help you,

miss?"

His eagerness reminded her of herself at that age. With a kind smile, she handed him Miz Georgia's list. "You may gather these items for me, and in the meantime, may I please speak with Mr. Polk."

"Sure thing." The boy showed her to the upstairs corridor. "Second door on the left."

Squaring her shoulders, Vera marched to the office door and peeked in. "Hello, Mr. Polk. Are you free to talk?"

His eyes lit up as he laid aside a pen. "Indeed I am. Do come in."

After accepting a glass of water and exchanging a few pleasantries, Vera cleared her throat. "You said you had a proposition for me."

"I do. However, it depends on whether we can settle on terms for the Beasley Mercantile."

Stating her answer was even harder than she'd expected. Lips pursed, she clutched her reticule. "As of this morning, I have determined the extent of the debts my father left behind, and it is sizable. The amount you are offering still leaves me owing a great deal to the bank as well as to our suppliers. Unless you increase your offer substantially, I don't know where the rest of the money will come from."

Seconds ticked by as Ephraim drummed his fingers on the desk. His mouth spread in the beginnings of a smile, and Vera couldn't tell whether it reflected greed or concern. Finally he spoke. "The economy being what it is, I am not in a position to increase my offer. However, as I told you on Sunday, I have an idea that could benefit us both."

"I'm listening."

"Our families have been acquainted for many years, so I'm well aware of your sewing skills. I also understand your schooling in Philadelphia included ladies' fashion design."

Curiosity aroused, Vera sat straighter. "That is correct."

"I would like to commission you to create my daughter's bridal gown and trousseau. In exchange, I will pay off an equivalent portion the Beasley Mercantile debt and apply your seamstress fees against it."

Lips pressed together, Vera mulled over the possibilities. She probably couldn't charge in Bryan what her services would fetch in Philadelphia, but it was a start. "We'd have all the terms in writing?"

"Naturally." Polk's grin widened. "Nancy's planning a Christmas wedding, which gives you not quite two months, but a supply of appropriate fabrics is already on order, and with your skills, I'm sure—"

"Two months? To design and sew a complete wedding ensemble?" Vera pressed her hands against the arms of the chair. "I'm good, but I'm not a miracle worker. Besides, I don't even own a sewing machine."

"I'll borrow one for you. I'll get you anything you need." Ephraim's tone had subtly shifted from confidence to desperation. "Please, Nancy's our only daughter, and she hasn't been happy with a single thing her mother has shown her from all those fancy catalogues."

Eyes closed, Vera breathed out slowly. With a sewing machine and no interruptions, she *might* be able to finish everything in time for a Christmas wedding. At a minimum, Nancy would have a lovely gown and traveling suit. But Vera's hopes of returning to her aunt and uncle in Philadelphia in time for the holidays would vanish, and the prospect of spending Christmas so far from the only family she had left was almost more than she could bear.

Before tears fell, she rose and hiked her chin. "I'll need a day or two to think this over." Then, halfway to the door, she stopped. Without turning around, she said, "In any case, you may have your attorney and banker prepare the necessary papers for the purchase of Beasley Mercantile."

Riding among the yearling heifers, Jacob slapped his lariat against his thigh. "Get on there, ladies. No dawdlin'." He looked toward neighboring rancher Ivan O'Dale, who leaned on the corral fence. "See any you like?"

"Over there with the stripe on her nose." The whiskered man pointed. "Bring her over for a closer look-see."

At the subtle shift of Jacob's weight, Curly responded instantly. Seconds later, the horse had expertly cut the heifer from the herd.

"She's a fine one," Jacob stated as Ivan gave the cow the once-over. "Out of our best breeding stock."

Ivan hemmed and hawed. "Price is kinda high, though." He tipped back his hat and grinned. "Tell you what. Throw in two more heifers and that old nag you're riding, and I'll tack on another hundred."

Laughing out loud, Jacob could only shake his head. "You never give up, do you? How many times will I have to tell you Curly isn't for sale?"

"Till you break down and sell her to me. Honest to Pete, that is the smartest, fastest, and downright prettiest cutting horse between here and the Red River."

Jacob never tired of the compliments Curly earned. After the war ended, he'd worked odd jobs while making his way home to Texas, and one old farmer had little to offer but hot meals and an empty barn stall to sleep in. He'd had a fine young filly, though, one he'd somehow managed to keep hidden while armies from both North and South were confiscating horses and mules for the war effort. Jacob had taken to the young horse right away, partly because her ribs stuck out worse than his own, partly because she was brighter than a newly minted nickel . . . and partly because of the fetching spiral curl in her forelock.

No denying it—from the first time Jacob saw the horse, she'd put him in mind of the pretty little "filly" he hoped would someday be his bride. When the farmer agreed to let Jacob have Curly in exchange for helping him get his crops in, it sure seemed like God was smiling on him.

He just hadn't expected to make it home to find Vera's family had shipped her off to Philadelphia.

But now she was back, and though the reason for her return was nothing Jacob would have wished upon her in a million years, he couldn't help hoping for a second chance to win her heart.

By mid-afternoon, Jacob had settled with Ivan O'Dale for six of the Richardson heifers. Sending Hector to the ranch with the remaining herd, Jacob detoured to Bryan to deposit the money into Miz Georgia's bank account.

Leaving the bank, he caught sight of a familiar profile through a café window across the street. Vera appeared engrossed in conversation with Nancy Polk, their heads bobbing as they studied something on the table between them. A fancy ladies' apparel catalogue, no doubt. Vera had announced over the weekend that she'd be designing Nancy's wedding trousseau.

Jacob heaved a hopeful sigh. Maybe this time next year—or sooner—Vera would be sewing her own wedding gown, while he got himself fitted for a spiffy suit and maybe even a top hat. A fine woman like Vera Mae Beasley deserved nothing less.

Sometime during his woolgathering, Vera and Nancy emerged from the café and now stood on the boardwalk saying their good-byes. A mess of papers and catalogues clutched to her bosom, Vera stepped to the rail where Miz Georgia's gentle buckskin, Dusty, was hitched. After tucking her things into a saddlebag, she set a foot in the stirrup and swung herself into the saddle.

Gracious, if she wasn't just as pretty on the back of a horse as she was in her Sunday finery! Gathering his wits, Jacob called her name and strode across the street.

With a surprised smile, Vera wheeled the horse around. "Jacob! I didn't expect you to be in town today."

"Had some business at the bank." He stood at Dusty's head, one hand on the bridle. "How's it going with Miss Polk?"

Vera glanced in the direction Nancy had gone, then gave her head a quick shake. "She's quite the pampered young lady. If I weren't desperately in debt, I'd back out of this arrangement before her demands drive me to the brink of insanity."

"Well, she is Ephraim Polk's daughter." Pretending to examine a fly bite on Dusty's neck, Jacob sidled closer. He was enjoying simply being in reaching distance of Vera's dainty leather boot. "Heading back to the ranch? Wait up while I get Curly and I'll ride with you."

As they set their horses on a leisurely pace toward a glorious November sunset, Vera described her afternoon with Nancy. "She certainly has good taste, and the gown she finally decided on will be stunning. But unless Ephraim is able to borrow a sewing machine for me, I'll be burning lanterns into the night to hand-stitch everything."

"I've heard of those newfangled Singer sewing machines. Bet they cost a pretty penny."

"A good one will run at least a hundred dollars." Vera's chest heaved. "My aunt in Philadelphia has the latest model, and it made sewing such a pleasure. I used it for all the gowns I made for my design classes."

An uneasy feeling settled in Jacob's belly. "Once you're done with Nancy's trousseau, I guess you'll be anxious to get back to Philly."

"I only wish I could count on returning by Christmas. But with the wedding, plus the Beasley Mercantile debts . . ." Shifting in the saddle, Vera brushed at something on her cheek. "I'm not sure when I'll ever be free to leave."

Jacob didn't mind at all that Vera might be around for a long time yet, but he sure hated seeing her so forlorn. Longing to reach over and comfort her, he nudged Curly closer. "I know how much you're grieving, but I promise, I'll do everything in my power to make your Christmas a happy one."

Her sad smile stabbed clean through his heart. "What would I do without you, Jacob?"

He hoped neither one of them had to find out.

CHAPTER FIVE

THE BUSY SUPPLY room at the rear of Ephraim's general store wasn't the most pleasant of places to design and sew a wedding trousseau, but at least Ephraim had set Vera up with a borrowed sewing machine and a sturdy oak worktable. Working behind the store also gave her ready access to the fabric, thread, and notions she would need.

The downside was her availability anytime Nancy came up with new ideas she wanted Vera to incorporate.

Well into her second week on the project, Vera had made good progress. As she sat at the sewing machine to stitch a shimmery white satin skirt panel, Ephraim peeked into the room.

"Sorry to interrupt," he said, holding aside the doorway curtain, "but I have a customer who'd like to speak with you."

Vera looked up to see a plump but fashionably attired matron step into the room. "I'm Tessie Arbuckle," the woman stated, "and I understand you're a dress designer—*exactly* what this town needs. Why, do you know I have to send all the way to Chicago or St. Louis for stylish apparel?" With a sidelong glance at Ephraim, she added, "It's shameful."

Brows lifted, Vera rose from her bench at the sewing machine and introduced herself. "Is there something I can do for you?"

"I'm hosting several distinguished guests for Thanksgiving dinner, so I'll need something fashionable to wear. I do hope you can fit me in."

Hands folded, Vera shot Ephraim a concerned glance. "I'm not sure I can, what with everything I must complete for Mr. Polk's daughter."

"Mrs. Arbuckle is one of our best customers." Ephraim gave a frantic nod. "Please, do whatever you must to meet her needs, even if it means delaying one or two of Nancy's requests."

Vera spent the next hour discussing patterns and fabric choices with Tessie Arbuckle. The woman had definite ideas but graciously listened to Vera's suggestions, and soon they'd agreed upon a design. Vera took measurements, and since they were pressed for time, Mrs. Arbuckle reluctantly settled for a lightweight maroon woolen fabric Ephraim currently had in stock. Vera promised to start on the dress by the weekend.

Gathering up her things, Mrs. Arbuckle beamed a smile. "The ladies of Bryan are so blessed to have you, my dear. Be assured, I'll recommend you to all my friends."

"Thank you, but—" Before Vera could protest that she had plenty to do for the Polk wedding, and furthermore, didn't plan to stay in Bryan any longer than necessary, Mrs. Arbuckle flounced from the room with a breezy wave.

Vera worked awhile longer on Nancy's wedding gown, then eased her tired shoulders and slipped on her coat for the ride back to the ranch. If she rented a room in town, she could add another couple of hours to her workday, but she couldn't afford the expense. Besides, the thought of sitting down to another of Miz Georgia's delicious hot meals made her stomach growl in anticipation.

The western sky had turned a brilliant shade of melon by the time Vera led Dusty into the barn. As she unbuckled the cinch to remove Dusty's saddle, Jacob strolled in.

"Let me help." In one smooth move, he hefted saddle and blanket and whisked them into the tack room. "How's the trousseau coming?"

"Fine." Vera eased off Dusty's bridle and handed it to Jacob. "Except now I have another client—and may be getting more." She described her visit with Tessie Arbuckle. "I love the work and can certainly use the money, but too many extra commitments will only delay my return to Philadelphia."

Turning away, Jacob silently hung up the bridle. When he stepped from the tack room, he asked softly, "Would sticking around here be so bad?"

His weak smile made Vera wish she hadn't spoken so honestly. After so many years apart, these last few weeks of getting reacquainted had been wonderful, but since she didn't plan to stay, she hadn't allowed herself to think beyond the immediate future and settling her family's estate. Had she missed obvious signs that Jacob wanted something more from her than friendship?

Suddenly tongue-tied, she grabbed a curry and busied herself brushing down the horse.

Jacob's hand on her forearm stilled her frenzied motion.

"Answer me, Vera. Can't you think of at least a few good things about being back in Texas?"

"Why, of course." She laughed nervously, her gaze fixed on his strong fingers. "There's, um . . ." How was she supposed to think while he stood so close? Masculine smells of leather and shaving soap nearly undid her.

Abruptly, she pulled away. "I should finish up here and see if Miz Georgia needs help with supper."

She dared not even glance at Jacob as she hurriedly brushed the sweat marks along Dusty's back. With the horse secured in a stall, Vera tossed in a flake of hay, checked the water pail, and then rushed to the house. Out of breath, she leaned against the closed kitchen door and waited for her heart to still.

"Dearie me, child." Miz Georgia turned from setting out plates and napkins. "You ran in here like the devil himself was after you."

No, but something almost as frightening. What she'd seen in Jacob's eyes a few moments ago, the longing, the hope—

"Miz Georgia . . ." Her voice quavered "I think Jacob is falling in love with me."

The white-haired woman laughed out loud. "Of course he is, you silly girl! You're just now figuring it out?"

Weak-kneed, Vera sank into the nearest chair. "Oh, dear, what shall I do?"

"All depends on whether you return those feelings." Miz Georgia sat facing Vera and gently took her hands. "Do you?"

Vera chewed her lip. "I—I don't know. I've been friends with Jacob since we were schoolchildren. I've never thought of him in any other way."

"Any reason why you can't?"

Squeezing her eyes shut briefly, Vera drew a deep breath. "There's one very big reason why I mustn't entertain such feelings. It wouldn't be fair to either of us when I return to Philadelphia."

"And you're dead set on going back?"

"My parents and brother are gone, and Ephraim Polk will soon own what's left of the mercantile." Vera shrugged. "Besides the debt my family left behind, there's nothing left for me here."

"I reckon if that's all you see, then you're probably right." Miz Georgia slowly pushed to her feet. "Best wash up for supper. The menfolk'll be in soon."

A new kind of sadness crept over Vera, along with questions she couldn't bring herself to answer.

When supper ended, Jacob stayed to help Miz Georgia with the dishes. He'd missed having Vera at the table, but Miz Georgia had said Vera was tired and decided to take a plate up to her room.

Jacob figured it was more than just fatigue. Earlier in the barn, he'd foolishly given her a glimpse into his heart, and now things had changed between them.

He dried the last plate and set it on a shelf, then prepared to say good night and head to the bunkhouse.

"Hold on, Jacob." Miz Georgia laid the dishcloth on the rim of the sink. "Pour yourself another cup of coffee and let's sit a spell."

"Somethin' on your mind?" he asked as he filled a mug.

"Same as what's on yours." She motioned him toward the parlor, and they sat in matching horsehair rockers facing the wood stove. A cozy, low-burning fire took the early-November chill off the room.

After a few minutes sipping coffee, Jacob heaved a sigh. No use pretending he didn't know what Miz Georgia was hinting at. "It's hopeless. She's going back to Philly first chance she gets."

"Yep, probably so." Miz Georgia nodded thoughtfully. "Unless somebody gives her a real good reason to stick around."

Jacob rubbed one thumb hard against the rocker arm. "In Philly, Vera was living in a fine home, wearing fine clothes, and getting all cultured with education and such. What could I offer her? Even if I convinced her to stay, it'll be years before I've put aside enough to give my bride a proper home."

Miz Georgia slanted him a disbelieving frown. "You've already forgotten about our agreement?"

"No, ma'am, but—" Jacob coughed nervously and set down his empty mug. After he'd been working for Miz Georgia for a few months, she'd come to him with a proposition. Being a widow and getting on in years, she knew there'd come a time when living on the ranch would no longer be sensible. Having no children to pass things on to, and with her growing affection for Jacob, she'd been holding back a portion of Jacob's wages every month toward eventually signing the property over to him.

"I'm not getting any younger, son." Miz Georgia rose stiffly and slid another log into the stove, then eased her back while soaking in the warmth. "Not that I'm in any hurry to while away my days in a rocking chair, but I'll be switched if I let you give up your girl just because you're currently sleeping in a bunkhouse with several other smelly cowpokes."

Jacob wasn't real sure what Miz Georgia was suggesting, but he knew enough not to argue. At any rate, he still had no idea how to go about winning Vera's heart, especially if she'd made up her mind to leave Texas.

Then another thought ambushed him. What if Vera had a beau back in Philly? She hadn't mentioned one, but then she'd been awfully preoccupied with settling her family's affairs and now sewing up a storm for the Polk wedding. If Vera had an understanding with a sophisticated city boy, Jacob might as well give up now.

He leaned forward, hands clasped between his knees as he looked up at Miz Georgia. "You ever heard Vera mention a . . . a suitor she might have left behind in Pennsylvania?"

"Nary a word." Miz Georgia cast him a knowing smile as she collected their empty cups. "Have a little faith in God's perfect plan and timing. He never disappoints."

Left alone in the darkened parlor, Jacob listened to the splash of water and clink of pottery as Miz Georgia finished in the kitchen, then the soft pad of her boots as she climbed the stairs. Eyes closed, he imagined someday sharing this house with Vera as his wife. The kitchen sounds, the light tread on the stairs, the lingering scent of lilacs when she passed through a room . . .

Tiredly, he rose and trudged out to the barn for a final check of the livestock before heading to the bunkhouse. When Curly nickered in her stall, Jacob walked over to give her ears a gentle rub and twine his fingers in her spiraling forelock. Not near as soft as he imagined Vera's curls to be, and it looked like he might never get the chance to find out.

Passing Dusty's stall, Jacob noticed Vera's leather folder lying on a hay bale. In such a hurry to escape, she must have forgotten about it. Maybe he shouldn't look inside, but he wanted to know everything there was to know about her, even if he didn't understand a thing about sewing pretty dresses. He lit an overhead lantern and then sat down on the bale. With the folder open across his lap, he paged slowly through sketches of bridal gowns, fancy dresses, and tailored skirts and blouses. Notations on each picture listed measurements, fabric types, colors, and other details only a seamstress would understand.

Then he came across a design that was clearly for a woman of portly build and rather more mature. Jacob squinted to read the notes—*Mrs. Tessie Arbuckle, must complete no later than Monday, Nov. 25, in time for Thanksgiving.*

Yep, now that Tessie had engaged Vera's services, it wouldn't be long before the woman started referring her friends. And the more sewing Vera did, the sooner she'd have her debts paid off.

And the sooner she'd leave for Philadelphia.

CHAPTER SIX

"I DON'T KNOW . . ." Tessie Arbuckle pivoted in front of the full-length mirror in her bedroom. "Do you think it makes me look a bit too busty?"

Having worked all weekend on Mrs. Arbuckle's dress, Vera had brought it over for a fitting. She clamped her lips together and forced a smile. It wouldn't do to tell a paying customer that certain aspects of her figure could not easily be disguised. She draped a lace-trimmed ivory collar across the bodice. "This helps, don't you agree? And the light color draws attention upward toward your face."

"Oh, yes, I see what you mean." Mrs. Arbuckle simpered at her reflection.

Vera could only laugh to herself as she bent to mark the hem. Another day or two and the dress would be finished, with plenty of time to spare before Thanksgiving—a good thing since Sunday at church Mrs. Arbuckle had introduced Vera to three other ladies, all eager to have Vera design something special for them. At least no one had urgent need of anything too complicated in time for the holidays. Vera still had much to do before Nancy Polk's wedding.

With Mrs. Arbuckle's dress tucked into a canvas garment bag, Vera hurried back to Polk's General Store. Thuds and loud voices from the supply room made her halt at the curtained doorway. With more merchandise arriving daily, Vera's workspace grew increasingly crowded. Her table and sewing machine were now shoved into a corner and surrounded by barrels and stacked crates.

Inhaling a sharp breath, she searched the store for Ephraim. When she spotted him helping a customer with a pair of boots, she stormed over. "This situation is untenable. I cannot sew under such cramped and noisy conditions."

"Pardon me, sir." Ephraim gave the customer an apologetic smile, then hooked his arm through Vera's and escorted her a short distance away. Voice tight and low, he stated, "It can't be helped. With the Christmas season approaching and Bryan's population growing every day, I need extra inventory on hand."

Vera shook off his hold and fisted her hips. "Then you'll have to find me another place to work."

"If I'd known you'd be this temperamental—"

"Excuse me? You're the one pushing me to finish your daughter's trousseau *and* referring your female customers with even more requests for my talents."

"I thought you'd be glad of the extra work." Ephraim narrowed one eye. "Are you forgetting those debts you so badly need to pay off?"

"Not for one moment." The reminder brought a clutch to Vera's throat. He was right—she couldn't afford to turn away business.

But she also couldn't continue working in a crowded supply room. "Perhaps we could move everything out to Mrs. Richardson's. My room there is spacious, and I'm far enough along on Nancy's wedding dress that I wouldn't need to see her as often for fittings."

Ephraim pondered the idea for a few moments before agreeing. "There is one problem, however. I arranged to borrow the sewing machine only until my daughter's wedding. It's fine for you to use it for your other sewing as time permits, but after the holidays, I'll have to return it."

Vera swallowed. Without a sewing machine she'd have a difficult time keeping up with dressmaking orders. Well, she'd just have to sew faster. "I understand. I'll ask Jacob to bring the buckboard tomorrow so we can move everything out to the ranch."

Jacob could tell by Vera's restless stance how hard it was to ask this favor. Since the other evening in the barn, she'd barely said ten words to him. Now she shifted before him on Miz Georgia's side porch, arms folded and head down.

"I do hate to bother you," she said for the third time. "It's just —"

"I said it's no bother, Vera." Impatience tinged his tone. He wanted to say he'd do backward somersaults if it would make her happy, but that might scare her off even worse. "I'll bring the wagon around after breakfast in the morning."

"Thank you, Jacob." She reached for the doorknob, then smiled timidly over her shoulder. "See you at supper."

Gracious, what one little smile could do to his insides! Watching her walk through the door was sheer torture, when he ached to take her in his arms and devour those lips until she begged for mercy.

Best to shake off such notions right now. He was about to head over to the bunkhouse to wash up for supper when Miz Georgia stepped onto the porch.

"Couldn't help overhearing," she said with a wink. "Having Vera right here at the ranch could be a real advantage for pursuing your cause."

Jacob gave a harsh laugh. "It's looking more and more like a *lost* cause, if you ask me."

"Looks can be deceiving." With a knowing grin, Miz Georgia went back inside.

After another quiet supper, Jacob rose to help with the dishes, but Miz Georgia stopped him. "Why don't you go on upstairs with Vera and see if you need to move some furniture around to make room for her sewing things."

Vera's wide-eyed stare mirrored Jacob's discomfort. "Ma'am—" His voice cracked. "That would hardly be proper."

"Fiddlesticks. You'll leave the door open, and I'll be right down here listening to every creak of the floorboards." Miz Georgia emptied a kettle of hot water into her dishpan, then waved them toward the stairs. "Go on, you two."

After a moment's hesitation, Vera started upstairs. Jacob hesitated a mite longer before following. Vera had a kerosene lamp lit by the time he caught up. Reflected back from the dresser mirror, the light bathed Vera's curls in a golden glow. She looked so pretty that Jacob almost couldn't breathe.

With a weak shrug, Vera motioned toward the window. "I'd like to put the sewing machine over there, where I can catch the daylight. But we might have to move the dresser to make room for the worktable."

Jacob rubbed his chin. "Let's see what we can do."

With the dresser shifted closer to the door and an upholstered chair moved from under the window to the opposite corner, Vera studied the arrangement. "I think this will work. Thank you."

"My pleasure." Jacob almost wished there was more furniture to move. He edged toward the door. "I should—"

"Wait. Don't go yet." Vera took a tiny step closer. Glancing away, she said softly, "Something's changed between us, and I don't like it."

Nerves on alert, Jacob spoke cautiously. "Can't say I like it much, myself."

"We used to be able to talk about anything, before . . ."

"Before I went off to war and then your folks sent you to Philly." Jacob examined a scuff mark on the toe of his boot. "Guess we've both been changed by our experiences."

"But does change have to mean we can no longer be friends?"

Jacob raised his head, one eye narrowed in a look that held all the feelings he couldn't express aloud. "I hope we'll always be friends, Vera Mae."

Abruptly, she turned away, one hand pressed to her mouth as a sob escaped. In an instant he was at her side, wrapping her in his arms and whispering comforting words against her hair.

Sniffling, Vera rested her forehead against his shirtfront. "Sometimes the grief sneaks up on me and I feel so alone . . . so horribly alone."

"You're not alone. And you never will be, if I've got any say in the matter." Holding her closer, Jacob stroked the silky curls he'd admired since he'd first learned to appreciate the amazing differences between boys and girls. "Vera . . ." He swallowed hard, forcing out his next words. "I want you to stay."

She tipped her head to meet his gaze and sucked in a tiny breath. "Jacob, what are you asking?"

He couldn't do this, not when she was still so vulnerable. Grasping her shoulders, he eased her from his embrace, then swiveled toward the darkened window and fought for control—something he had precious little of when in the presence of Vera Mae Beasley. "I, uh, just meant I want you to stay here at the ranch as long as you need to. Miz Georgia's glad to help and glad for the company."

When she didn't speak for several seconds, Jacob wondered if she'd left him alone in the room. Then he felt her hand slide into his as she stated firmly, "We have to stop this."

He slid his gaze toward her. "Stop what?"

"Watching our words around each other." Her voice softened even more, until he wasn't quite sure he heard her. "Not saying what's on our hearts."

Lifting her hand, he studied each dainty fingertip, then laced his fingers through hers. He dared a glance at her huge brown eyes, still moist from tears. "I think by now you know what's on my heart."

"Jacob . . ." Her free hand crept up to cradle his cheek, and he could die of sheer pleasure at the feel of her warm, tender touch.

"I don't think you should talk anymore, Vera Mae, because . . ." He bent closer, his arms enfolding her. "Because I'm about to kiss you, and nothing in this world is gonna stop me."

Nothing in the world could stop Vera from snaking her arms around Jacob's strong, solid shoulders and returning his kiss with all the passion she'd been holding inside. His love was a comfort, a fortress against the grief and despair of the past several weeks.

Tasting the salt of her tears along with the sweetness of his mouth, Vera trembled and drew back. "Jacob, I can't. This is pure torture for me, but we just can't let this happen."

"Why not?" A harshness had crept into his tone. "I love you, Vera Mae. Always have, always will."

"I care deeply for you, too—more than I ever let myself imagine until now." She clutched his sleeves in a desperate attempt to make him understand. "But I can't continue living off the charity of friends. If I return to Philadelphia, I'll have a much better chance of finding employment as a designer of ladies' fashions. It's my dream, what my parents sacrificed to give me. I can't let them down."

Hips cocked, Jacob hauled in a long breath. "Hasn't it occurred to you that a growing town like Bryan has need of your talents? Look at all the business you're already getting."

"I know, but you're forgetting one thing." Vera paced to the empty space in front of the window. "When I finish Nancy's trousseau, the sewing machine goes back. And a seamstress without a sewing machine is like a . . . a cowhand without a horse."

After a long, tense pause, Jacob replied, "I see your point."

"Do you?" Vera pivoted to face him, her gaze pleading. "Papa always said that once I got my schooling out east, he'd set me up with my own fashion department at the mercantile." Her tone grew wistful. "He just knew with the railroad coming to Millican and the town growing by leaps and bounds, that ladies for miles around would come to the Beasley Mercantile to have me make their dresses. But that was before—" She broke off as the reality of what had happened to her town and her family crashed in on her all over again.

"Aw, Vera." Jacob held her close once more and graced the top of her head with a tender kiss. "Don't give up. Your dream can still come true. Maybe not exactly like you hoped, but if this is God's plan for you, He'll make it happen."

Vera nodded against Jacob's chest. She wasn't certain she shared his conviction, but she wanted to.

She also realized she wanted to stay right here in the shelter of his arms for the rest of her life.

CHAPTER SEVEN

AT THE GENERAL store the next morning, Jacob sent Vera to the supply room to pack up her sewing things and then cornered Ephraim Polk out front. "How long would it take to order a sewing machine?"

Ephraim gave his jaw a thoughtful rub. "A few weeks at least."

"Can you find out and let me know? If there's a chance of getting it here by Christmas, I'd be much obliged."

Laying a catalogue on the counter, Ephraim opened it to pictures of sewing machines. "Pick the one you want and I'll see what I can do."

They all looked the same to Jacob. He shrugged. "Which one's best?"

A knowing grin stole across Ephraim's face as he pointed to one of the pictures. "I'd go with this one. Latest model from Singer." He studied the fine print. "Looks like if I wire an order today, they can ship it out immediately. I'd need a deposit up front, though."

Jacob tugged his wallet from his back pocket and counted out some bills. "This is all I can give you for now. I'll have the rest by the time it gets here."

Ephraim leaned an elbow on the counter. "Normally I'd ask for half now and half on delivery, but since I suspect this is for a certain young lady . . ."

"Please don't say anything to Vera. I want it to be a surprise."

"You have my word." Ephraim made a lock-and-key motion at his lips.

Leaving Ephraim to place the order, Jacob marched to the supply room. He found Vera wrapping some shimmery satin cloth in a protective layer of brown paper.

"This about does it," she said as she laid the fabric in a crate. "These three boxes go, plus the table and sewing machine."

Jacob had left the buckboard near the rear door. After carrying out the crates, he snagged one of Ephraim's young store clerks to help carry the table and sewing machine. Soon everything was loaded and they headed back to the ranch.

They hadn't gone far when Vera casually mentioned, "I noticed you and Ephraim with your heads together earlier."

Jacob clicked his tongue, encouraging the horses into a faster gait. "Just ordering a few things I need."

"That's all? You looked so serious."

Not near as serious as what was going through Jacob's mind while Vera's hip brushed his with every bounce of the wagon seat. After their kiss last night, he still tasted her sweet lips and hoped they'd have another opportunity very, very soon. With a nervous laugh, he brought his attention back to their conversation. "Serious? No, just making sure ol' Ephraim didn't overcharge me."

"Ephraim's a shrewd businessman, but I will say he's an honest one." At a northerly gust of wind, Vera drew her wool shawl closer about her shoulders. "I've gone over and over the figures he offered for the mercantile, and though I wish it were more, I believe he's been quite fair."

"So y'all have settled on terms?"

"And the money's in the bank." Vera huffed. "Well, it *was* in the bank, until I applied it to the bills I owe." Shifting, she tucked her arm through Jacob's. "But let's not talk about it anymore. I need to stop dwelling on what was and start looking toward the future."

Jacob liked the sound of that. He also liked how close she was sitting. And he sure hoped the future she had in mind included him.

Arriving at the ranch, Jacob enlisted Esteban's help in getting Vera's sewing things upstairs. No chance of stealing a kiss with Esteban around and Miz Georgia volunteering to help Vera arrange her supplies. Deciding he'd best get on with work he knew something about, namely cattle ranching, Jacob sent Esteban out to the range and then retreated to his tiny office at one end of the bunkhouse. Jacob would much rather ride herd with his men, but unfortunately, a ranch foreman's job involved a certain amount of desk work.

And every time he sat down to update his tally books and ledgers, Jacob couldn't resist peeking at the little notebook where he tracked how much of his salary Miz Georgia laid aside each month toward the purchase of the ranch. Except it was too much like the old saying, "A watched pot never boils," because despite the generously low selling price Miz Georgia had agreed to, Jacob's savings sure didn't seem to grow very fast.

And now he'd gone and ordered a top-of-the-line Singer sewing machine for Vera, which meant less going into his ranch savings. He supposed a few months longer wouldn't hurt anything. For now, his main goal was convincing Vera she didn't have to return to Philly. If she stayed, he'd have plenty of time to court her while putting aside enough so he could eventually give his bride the home she deserved.

On the Monday before Thanksgiving, Vera rode to town to deliver Tessie Arbuckle's dress. Tessie oohed and aahed and claimed it was the most flattering style she'd ever worn. As she paid Vera the amount due, she promised again to refer all her friends. "And I have a passel of them! Once they get an eyeful of this fancy frock, they'll be beating a path to your door."

The only problem was, Vera's "door" for the time being was several miles outside of town, not exactly convenient for the regular fittings designing a dress required. She may have Nancy Polk's trousseau well underway, but new customers would require much more attention, and every hour of travel devoured another hour of sewing time.

Maybe moving her sewing to Miz Georgia's hadn't been such a smart idea after all.

It certainly was peaceful, though, without the constant noise and interruptions she'd endured in Ephraim's supply room. And she did enjoy looking out her window and catching glimpses of Jacob at work. Oh, how she'd miss him when the Polk wedding was behind her and she returned to Philadelphia!

"Vera . . . I want you to stay."

If he only knew how much she wanted to! But nothing could restore her family or Beasley Mercantile or the plans and dreams her parents had nurtured in her since childhood. She was on her own now, and even if she must live with her aunt and uncle awhile longer, she refused to be a burden. She *must* find the means to support herself.

Returning to the ranch, she found Miz Georgia slicing cold roast beef for sandwiches. "What can I do?" Vera asked as she laid her things on a chair.

"Bread's buttered, water's poured, table's set. Everything's almost ready." Miz Georgia abruptly laid down the knife, then shook out her fingers and released a muted groan.

Vera rushed over. "Did you cut yourself?"

"No, no. It's this cussed ol' arthritis." She glanced out the window. "Must be a storm brewing. My joints can always tell."

Vera hated to mention she hadn't seen a cloud in the sky all morning. "Go sit down. I'll finish here." Retrieving the knife, she watched with concern as Miz Georgia shuffled to the table. Most days the spry little woman bounced around like someone half her age.

Miz Georgia stretched out one leg and massaged her knee. "How'd Tessie like her dress?"

"She was delighted." Vera laid another slice of roast on the plate. "And now I can return my full attention to Nancy's wedding. I still have so much to do!"

"I'd offer to help with the hemming and such, but as you can see, these old hands aren't up to such fine work anymore." Regret tinged Miz Georgia's tone. "Truth is, I fear my days on this ranch are numbered."

Alarm raced up Vera's spine. "Don't say such things. You have many good years ahead."

"I do hope you're right." Miz Georgia gave a weak chuckle. "But I'm looking forward to a cozy little house in town someday and leaving the ranch in more capable—and much younger—hands."

Vera carried the platter of sliced roast beef to the table, and together she and Miz Georgia made sandwiches with the buttered bread. Curious, Vera asked, "Do you have family who'll take over the ranch for you?"

"My husband and I never had children of our own. Biggest heartbreak of my life." She shook her head sadly before casting Vera a contented smile. "But the biggest blessing of my widowed years is Jacob Collins. You won't find a finer man anywhere."

Heart clenching in silent agreement, Vera laid another sandwich on a plate. Then understanding dawned. "You're planning to turn the ranch over to Jacob?"

"In due time. We have an arrangement." Miz Georgia rose with pained slowness. "Best call the men in for lunch."

Shortly, the ranch hands who weren't out on the range gathered at the table. Vera continued to be impressed that Miz Georgia insisted on feeding the men in her own kitchen instead of letting them cook for themselves or, at the very least, sending their meals out to the bunkhouse.

As always, Jacob took a seat at the head of the table, with Miz Georgia at the opposite end. For the first time, Vera noticed how natural and right it seemed, now that she knew the ranch would be Jacob's one day. Coming home to nothing after the war, he deserved this blessing, and so much more.

I want to bless you, too, a soft voice spoke in Vera's spirit, and along with it, a verse from Proverbs came to mind: *For surely there is an end; And thine expectation shall not be cut off.*

An end to the tears, the expectation of better things to come? Vera could only pray God came through on His promises soon.

Though she could ill afford the time off, Vera decided she'd do no sewing on Thanksgiving Day. Instead, she rose early to help Miz Georgia stuff the turkey and bake pies. Working alongside the elderly woman brought back sweet memories of Vera's childhood and helping her mother prepare the holiday feast.

After trimming the pie crusts, Miz Georgia laid the leftover strips on a baking pan, then spread them with melted butter and sprinkled cinnamon sugar over the top . . . just like Mama used to do. Eyes welling, Vera turned aside and dabbed her cheeks with her apron hem.

Miz Georgia encircled Vera's waist and gave her a squeeze. "First holiday without your loved ones is terrible hard, don't I know."

"I feel so silly crying over scraps of pie crust. I don't want to imagine how hard Christmas will be."

"We'll take care of you, honey. Don't you worry." With a quick pat on Vera's shoulder, Miz Georgia returned to her bakin

By *we*, Vera felt pretty sure the kindly woman referred t

and Jacob. Vera hadn't told either of them yet that she'd inquired in town yesterday about train tickets to Philadelphia. If all went well, she'd complete Nancy's trousseau a few days before Christmas and then be on her way. Aunt Cassandra and Uncle Reggie would never replace Vera's parents, but what was Christmas without family? Difficult as the holiday was bound to be, at least she'd have the distraction of her two married cousins and their lively children ripping away wrapping paper and exclaiming over their gifts.

The thought reminded Vera she couldn't return to Philadelphia empty-handed. Since she didn't have extra money to purchase Christmas gifts, she could use fabric scraps to create small treasures her aunt, uncle, and cousins would enjoy. Perhaps a satin pillow, a keepsake bag, an embroidered apron . . .

Letting her imagination run free, she occupied her hands paring and slicing potatoes. With the potatoes on the stove to boil, she helped to lay the table with Miz Georgia's crisp linen tablecloth, fine china, and silver. A bouquet of yellow and orange chrysanthemums served as the centerpiece.

The delicious dinner, combined with the lively conversations bouncing around the table, kept Vera from dwelling too much on missing her family. Jacob and the ranch hands pitched in for cleanup duty, while Vera helped Miz Georgia pack a large hamper with turkey, side dishes, and pie to be delivered to the men out on the range.

When at last the kitchen had been put in order, Jacob drew Vera aside. "Take a walk with me?"

Still feeling stuffed, Vera set a hand on her abdomen. "A walk would be lovely."

After she hung up her apron, Jacob draped her heavy wool shawl around her shoulders, and they stepped outside into a sunny but breezy afternoon. They hadn't gone but a few steps when Jacob reached for her hand.

Beyond the barn and corral, they followed a meandering path through brushy grasses and mesquite trees. Near a shallow creek, a thick tree branch growing low to the ground made a perfect spot to sit and rest. With the breeze tugging at Vera's shawl, she welcomed Jacob's sheltering arm.

Her gaze combed the grassy plain, with clumps of twisted trees here and there but not a hill or ridge as far as the eye could see. "It's beautiful," she murmured, "in a wild sort of way."

"Yes, it is." Jacob smoothed a windblown curl from her eyes, and she realized he'd been looking straight at her.

Heat rose in her cheeks. She fumbled with her hair to pin back the loosened strands.

"Don't." Jacob gently lowered her hands and held them firmly in his lap. "I like your hair down and messy, those springy curls all in a tangle." His tone had gone soft and breathless. When he reached up to twine his fingers in her hair, her own breath stilled in her lungs.

He was going to kiss her again, and she wanted him to. Desperately.

Then, with his mouth only inches from hers, he drew back. So stunned by what *didn't* happen, she tipped forward, nearly falling off the branch.

Jacob steadied her as he stood. "We should head back."

"But it's still early. And I thought . . ." *I thought you were going to kiss me, and now I can't bear it if you don't.*

As if he'd read her mind, Jacob gave his head a sad shake. "Guess it's pretty clear I have designs on you, Vera Mae Beasley, and we dare not stay out here alone and unchaperoned a moment longer."

CHAPTER EIGHT

WALKING VERA BACK to the house felt like the longest journey of Jacob's life. His longing to kiss her nearly leveled him, but he knew once his lips touched hers, he might not be able to stop.

After he'd delivered her safely into Miz Georgia's care, he hurried out to his office in the bunkhouse. Even if it was a holiday, better to stay occupied with ranch business than to accept Miz Georgia's invitation to join her and Vera for another serving of pie. Because not even Miz Georgia's creamy pumpkin pie could possibly taste as sweet as Vera's kiss.

With Vera hard at work on Nancy Polk's wedding gown and other items of feminine apparel, Jacob stayed as busy as possible on Friday and Saturday so as not to be tempted to interrupt her. He could hardly wait for Sunday morning and their weekly drive into town for worship.

Except Vera seemed unusually quiet all morning, and Jacob was worried. As they ambled out of church after the service, he drew her aside. "You feelin' okay? You're not working yourself sick, are you?"

She looked up at him with a feeble smile. "No, just

preoccupied." Glancing toward the street, she chewed her lip. "There's something I really must do, but I don't know if I have the strength."

Jacob could see the hesitancy in her eyes. "What is it, Vera? Maybe I can help."

"It's time to . . ." With a subtle tremor in her chin, she straightened. "Time to see to things at home."

"Home. You mean in Millican."

She nodded. "It's been too hard to even think about, but I know I need to sort through everything. If I can sell the house, the furniture, and anything else of value, I'll be that much closer to settling my debts."

And going back to Philadelphia. Jacob tried not to show his disappointment. "I'll help any way I can."

"Thank you."

"How soon do you want to start?"

"Tomorrow, I think. I've finished Nancy's wedding gown and one of the other dresses she asked for. Now that I have a good start on the next items, I can spare a few days."

Before Jacob could help Vera into the seat, Miz Georgia caught up with them, two other church ladies in tow. "There you are, Vera. I'd like you to meet Jenny Drexler and Constance Kimball. They'd like to talk to you about designing some dresses for them."

Jacob gladly stepped out of the way. The more sewing Vera took on, the longer she'd need to stay in Bryan. He half listened as the ladies described their requests while Vera nodded and replied with comments about gores and gussets and piping and interfacing.

"You know," Mrs. Kimball stated, tapping Vera's arm, "you should open a dressmaking shop right here in town. The way Bryan is growing, you'd never lack for business."

Keep talking, Jacob wanted to shout.

"I appreciate your confidence," Vera said. She glanced at Jacob as if seeking his support. Or perhaps his understanding. "But I couldn't possibly, not with my other obligations."

When the ladies became insistent, Miz Georgia interrupted. "Now, Jenny, Constance, don't pester the poor girl. She's still getting her bearings after losing her family."

"Indeed." Mrs. Drexler looked appropriately regretful. "It's awful how many lives have been lost to the yellow fever. My heart goes out to you, sweetheart."

Seeing Vera's eyes well, Jacob decided it was time to head home. He took Vera's elbow. "Ladies, you won't mind finishing your sewing talk another time, will you? I can smell Miz Georgia's pot roast from here."

When they'd started on their way, Vera cast Jacob a grateful smile. "If I had the time, I wouldn't mind taking on more sewing for the ladies in town—heaven knows I can use the money. But all this talk of opening a shop? Even if I decided to stay in Bryan awhile, I simply don't have the means."

Miz Georgia, seated on Vera's other side, patted Vera's hand. "You're welcome to stay on with me for as long as you like. But I think you'd do right well with a shop in town. Just look at all the customers already lining up to have you design them a 'Vera Mae Beasley' original."

"You're forgetting one thing," Vera stated. "Once I finish

Nancy's wedding clothes, the sewing machine goes back. I'm working in the other orders as quickly as I can while I still have use of it."

Jacob bit the inside of his cheek to keep from blurting out his surprise. He still needed to scrape up the money he'd owe once the sewing machine came in. He could only pray this gift would convince Vera to stay in Texas long enough for him to win her heart and propose.

Early Monday morning, with Vera driving the buckboard and Jacob riding alongside on Curly, they left for Millican. Vera hated taking Jacob away from his ranch work, but he claimed he needed to pick up a bull calf from a rancher down that way and said the timing of her trip couldn't be better.

She suspected he was only humoring her.

Still, as she stood on the front porch of her childhood home, she was grateful not to face this moment alone.

"It looks so dreary," she murmured, one hand on the knob.

Jacob rested his hand atop hers, his touch gently reassuring. "You can do this."

As she stepped inside, memories washed over her, along with a flood of grief so great she feared she'd drown. If not for Jacob's strong arms surrounding her, she might have collapsed.

"Come sit down. I'll get you some water." Jacob guided her into the parlor, where she sank onto a sheet-covered chair.

All the furnishings were draped in dust protectors, she noticed absently. Who had gone to so much trouble—neighbors, perhaps?

She must thank them.

Jacob returned with a glass of water. "Kitchen pump still works. I let it run awhile to clear the sediment."

When she'd taken several sips, she smiled up at Jacob. "I'll be fine. Go take care of your business."

"I'm not leaving you alone. Just tell me what I can do."

Vera could see it would be pointless to argue, and besides, once she decided on what to keep and what to part with, there'd be some heavy lifting. Miz Georgia had already told Vera she could use the barn loft to store anything she chose to keep. "All right, then. Let's start upstairs and work our way down."

By evening, Vera's shoulders ached from moving boxes and furniture, and her head throbbed from holding back tears. As she helped Jacob maneuver a cast-iron bed frame downstairs, a knock sounded on the front door. Dusting off her hands, Vera composed herself to answer.

It was Kathryn Stone from two houses down, and she carried a gingham-covered hamper. "Saw y'all working hard over here and thought I'd bring you a meal. So sorry about your family, Vera. I lost my Edward to the yellow fever. It's been a terrible, terrible time."

"Oh, Kathryn, you poor dear." Savory smells of roast chicken and vegetables wafted from the hamper, and Vera only then realized how hungry she was. "This is so thoughtful of you. Come in and I'll clear a space on the dining table. Will you stay and eat with us?"

"I hoped you'd ask. I've been watching for you to come home so we'd have a chance to talk."

Vera sent Jacob to fetch dishes from the kitchen, then helped Kathryn arrange things on the table while confiding how hard it had been to face this task. "Georgia Richardson offered to take me in—a true blessing—and then Ephraim Polk commissioned me to design and sew Nancy's trousseau, so I've hardly had a moment to think about"—with a sweep of her hand, she heaved a tired sigh—"all this."

"That's partly what I wanted to talk with you about." As they sat down to Kathryn's delicious meal, she explained that her son and daughter-in-law had decided to move back to Millican to take care of her in her widowhood. "My place is too small for their growing family, and I wondered if you'd consider selling them your house. They'd need some furniture, too, if you're of a mind to part with a few things."

Vera felt such relief that she wanted to cry all over again. "Nothing would make me happier. In fact, it would be an answered prayer."

After they'd put away leftovers and washed up the dishes, Vera showed Kathryn the furnishings and other items she didn't plan to keep. Soon they'd agreed upon a fair sales price, and Kathryn said she'd get a letter off to her son right away.

Returning to the parlor after seeing Kathryn out, Vera found Jacob staring into space, chin in his hands. He straightened and cast her a halfhearted smile. "Guess this arrangement will speed your return to Philly."

"It will certainly help. At the rate Millican is declining, I feared no one would ever want this house."

Jacob rose with a solemn nod. "It's getting late. I should mosey on over to the rooming house. You be all right here by yourself?"

"Actually, Kathryn invited me to spend the night with her, so you're welcome to sleep here if you like."

Vera was acutely aware of Jacob's silence as he walked her over to Kathryn's. How could she not notice how subdued he became at every mention of her return to Philadelphia? Yet how could she possibly stay? Selling the family home would allow her to pay back the mortgage her father had taken out, but she still had the store debts to settle.

If only she had the means to open her own shop as Miz Georgia's friends had urged. But almost every penny she made as a seamstress had to go straight to her creditors. She had nothing left to purchase a sewing machine, much less to lease shop space.

At Kathryn's door, Jacob looked as if he wanted to kiss her good night. She held her breath, wishing he would. Then the door burst open, and they both jumped back.

"Dear me," Kathryn said with a hand to her throat, "I appear to have interrupted something." Eyebrows raised, she smiled knowingly. "Don't mind me, you two. Vera, just let yourself in when you're ready." She quietly closed the door.

Looking everywhere but at Jacob, Vera hugged herself. "I suppose I should go inside. Thank you again for—"

"Vera." The desperate sound of Jacob's voice silenced her. Head down, he took both her hands in his. "Please. Don't go."

He shouldn't beg, but he couldn't help himself. The more time they spent together, the more deeply in love Jacob fell, and the idea of being separated from her ripped through his gut like being gored by Miz Georgia's prize bull.

"Jacob . . ." Vera's voice shook, and he hated himself for making her cry again. "Don't you know I'd stay if I could? But I just don't see any hope. By the end of the year I won't even have my family home anymore."

"But Miz Georgia said you could stay with her as long as you want. And anyway—" He clamped his lips together. Too soon to bring up marriage or the fact that eventually the Richardson spread would be his. "And anyway," he continued, changing course, "you need to have a little faith. The Good Book says, 'Now faith is the substance of things hoped for, the evidence of things not seen.' Neither one of us can see the future, but we can't give up hope that God's going to do a good thing in our lives."

Freeing one hand, she brushed at the wetness on her cheeks. "I want to have faith—truly, I do. But I'm just so tired."

Jacob's chest ached to see the strain etching her features. Everything she'd suffered, the time and effort she put into her sewing, all the work they'd done today at her house—no wonder exhaustion had taken its toll. He drew her into his arms and stroked her curls, every bit as silky as he'd imagined. "Then rest, Vera Mae. Rest and let me take care of you."

He lost track of how long they stood there, a quarter-moon creeping across the evening sky. He only knew how good it felt to hold her, to feel her lean into his strength. When she stirred and lifted her head, a languid smile graced her pink lips, and he bent low to taste lightly of their sweetness. "Go inside and get some sleep," he whispered. "I'll see you in the morning."

Back at Vera's house, Jacob found a couple of quilts and bundled up on one of the mattresses upstairs. Drifting off, he dreamed of waking with Vera in his arms and how happy they'd be someday as husband and wife.

CHAPTER NINE

"IT'S ALL STUNNING, Vera. Everything's just as I pictured!" Nancy Polk twirled in the crimson ball gown Vera had just completed. A lacy drop-shouldered wedding gown hung on the wardrobe door, and a riding skirt and velvet-trimmed waistcoat lay across the bed.

"I'll finish your traveling suit next," Vera said as she adjusted the flounce on Nancy's skirt. Straightening, she hid a grimace at the constant tightness in her shoulders from too many hours hunched over her sewing. Memories of being comforted in Jacob's arms a few nights ago made her long for his tender touch.

He'd spoken that night of hope, of trusting God for their future. *Their future.* Hers and Jacob's, together—and she knew with more certainty every day that nothing would make her happier. But how could she think about the future when her present was so fraught with difficulty?

At her dressing table, Nancy selected a jeweled necklace and held it to her throat. "Damon will simply swoon when he sees me in this dress on New Year's Eve. We're going to have such a grand party."

"I'm sure." Vera smiled politely. Nancy's intended, Damon West, was a young doctor who'd recently opened a practice in Bryan. Nancy had insisted her new wardrobe must befit a lady of such high social standing.

As Vera helped Nancy out of the ball gown, Nancy shot her a concerned glance. "Are you sure you'll have time to finish everything I've requested before the wedding? Rumor has it you've taken on sewing from other ladies around town."

"Just one or two." *Or three or four.* "Your trousseau is my top priority, though. I won't let the other orders interfere."

Vera said her good-byes, then stopped at Polk's General Store to select some fabric and notions before rushing back to the ranch. She'd have to work nonstop and limit her trips to town if she wanted to stay on schedule. With apologies to Miz Georgia for not being more helpful in the kitchen, she shut herself away upstairs with the ever-growing list of tasks she must complete by Christmas.

Working on Nancy's dresses during the day and spending a few hours each evening on the designs for Miz Georgia's church friends, Vera forged ahead. On Sunday morning, she prayed God would forgive her for not honoring the Sabbath, but after her journey to Millican last week, she couldn't afford one more day off.

By the following Saturday, and with Nancy's wedding only one week away, Vera felt ready to collapse. She'd completed Nancy's lined wool traveling suit and had started on an elaborate day dress that would require another fitting appointment. While in town, Vera also planned to deliver the dress she'd finished for

Mrs. Drexler, the money from which would go straight to the Beasley Mercantile creditor who'd recently sent an unpleasant letter demanding payment.

Vera was about to attach the second sleeve to Nancy's dress and then—

"Oh, no. No, no, no!"

Miz Georgia's worried voice echoed from downstairs. "Vera? Are you all right?"

Too upset to reply, Vera could only stare in disbelief at the sewing machine. She'd barely set the needle in place and started the treadle when everything jammed.

The door flew open and Miz Georgia rushed in. "Honey, what's wrong?"

"How could I have been so stupid!" Pushing her chair back, Vera pounded her forehead with clenched fists. She knew better than to sew over a pin, and yet she'd been in too big a hurry to remove it as she worked her way around the sleeve opening. Now she'd bent the needle and locked the gears.

Miz Georgia examined the machine while patting Vera's back. "I'll holler for Jacob. Maybe he can fix the confounded thing."

While Vera fumed and prayed she'd wake up from this living nightmare, Miz Georgia hurried to find Jacob and soon returned with him.

"Hey, now, it can't be that bad." He knelt beside Vera's chair, his gentle hand at her nape instantly soothing her.

"I'm afraid it is." Hiccupping a breath, Vera pointed to the machine. "I've broken it. How will I ever finish everything now?"

Nearly an hour later, Jacob still hadn't unjammed the sewing machine. He'd finally convinced Vera to go down to the kitchen with Miz Georgia and have a cup of tea. The sound of her whimpers and muttered curses—words he never imagined Vera even knew!—was too darned distracting.

He steeled himself with a slow, deep breath before traipsing downstairs with the bad news.

As he rounded the doorway into the kitchen, Vera's head sprang up. "Did you—"

He shook his head.

She burst into tears.

"There, there, honey." Miz Georgia enfolded Vera in her arms while shooting Jacob a frustrated glare.

"I tried everything I could think of, but fixing a sewing machine is a whole lot different from roping and branding a steer."

"What'll I do?" Vera wailed. "It's bad enough I can't finish all those dresses, but now I'll have to pay for ruining the sewing machine."

Seeing Vera so distraught made Jacob want to race out and scour the countryside for another sewing machine. Surely someone else in Brazos County owned one. Least he could do was ride into town and start asking around. He motioned Miz Georgia aside to tell her so.

"Good idea," she said, adding quietly, "but don't let on to Ephraim yet. No sense upsetting Nancy this close to the wedding."

Leaving Miz Georgia to comfort Vera, Jacob saddled Curly and rode fast and hard to Bryan. His first stop was Polk's General Store, where he made a casual inquiry about the Singer sewing machine he'd ordered for Vera. *Dear Lord, if there's any way You could get it here a couple weeks early, I'd sure be grateful.*

Ephraim reviewed the purchase order. "Sure, I'll check on it. Give me an hour or so to wire the manufacturer."

In the meantime, Jacob stopped in to see his pastor—more to the point, his pastor's wife. No one knew more about the goings-on around town than Helen Hicks.

"I'm afraid I can't be of much help finding a sewing machine," she told Jacob over apple pie and coffee he couldn't refuse. "But I know several ladies who are skilled with needle and thread. I'm sure they'd be pleased to help Vera Mae with hand-sewing whatever she needs."

"Thank you, ma'am. If it comes to that, I'll sure take you up on the offer." Jacob scraped the last bite of pie off his plate and washed it down with coffee. "But for now, this is just between you and me, all right?"

Back at the general store, he signaled Ephraim over to the counter. "Find out anything?"

"It's on a train somewhere between Knoxville and Memphis and should be here in plenty of time for Christmas." Ephraim grinned as if he'd just delivered the best possible news.

Jacob had been hoping for something better. "The machine you borrowed for Vera—mind if I ask where you found it?"

"It's on loan from a Houston garment firm I do business with. The rental is costing me a pretty penny, I might add." Ephraim's grin faded. "I'm sorely tempted to ask Vera for a percentage of her profits on those dresses she's sewing for other clients. She's *supposed* to be using the machine for my daughter's trousseau."

No wonder Ephraim Polk had become one of the richest businessmen in the county.

Didn't appear Jacob would have any luck unearthing another sewing machine on such short notice. He made tracks back to the Hicks home and told Helen to begin gathering her crew. "The sooner y'all can skedaddle on out to the Richardson place, the better. I've got one unhappy little lady sorely in need of your help."

Knowing Miz Georgia would insist on feeding their newly engaged seamstresses, Jacob made one more trip to the general store to purchase a few groceries. Ephraim must soon be told about the sewing machine, but better to wait until Vera could also assure him Nancy's wardrobe would be completed on time.

Then, riding out to the ranch, Jacob decided to make one more stop. The idea he'd been mulling over for days could no longer wait.

Miz Georgia peered out the kitchen window. "Someone's riding up in a buggy."

"Who is it?" Still wallowing in despair, Vera hardly looked up from the skirt hem she'd been hand-stitching. At least it was small progress.

"Well, I'll be!" Miz Georgia yanked open the door, letting in a chilly breeze. "It's Helen Hicks and some of her friends."

The pastor's wife? Here? Vera laid her sewing on the table and stood to tidy her hair. After all her blubbering, she must look a fright.

Minutes later, Mrs. Hicks and three friends bustled into the kitchen. "Don't you worry about a thing, dearie." Grasping Vera's hand, the pastor's wife related her conversation with Jacob. "So you just tell us what needs doing. We all know how to sew, and we're here to help."

Stunned speechless, Vera could only gape, until Miz Georgia stepped in and directed everyone upstairs. She took Vera by the arm. "Come now, honey, don't look a gift horse in the mouth. You get the ladies started stitching while I bake some cookies and brew a fresh pot of coffee." Miz Georgia gave her a nudge toward the stairs. "Best quit lollygagging."

By the time Vera made it upstairs, Mrs. Hicks and her friends were busily examining the garments Vera had been working on. One of the women had already sat down with needle, thread, and thimble to finish attaching the sleeve that had turned Vera's carefully ordered world upside-down.

Mrs. Hicks began gathering items into Vera's sewing basket. "We're going to need more chairs, dear. I suggest we take everything to the parlor."

So down again they went, and soon all the ladies had settled near the parlor windows for best light. With Vera directing their work while finishing the skirt hem she'd begun, the ladies chatted amiably as they stitched—a regular old-fashioned sewing bee. As the hours passed, every stitch brought Vera's designs closer to completion, and she felt her spirits lifting. That Jacob would go to such trouble to find help warmed her heart toward him even more.

She was falling in love—deeply in love with the boy-turned-man who clearly would do anything for her.

Vera had just returned from upstairs with the fabric pieces for one of Nancy's day dresses when Miz Georgia carried in a platter of cookies.

"Jacob's back," the woman stated as she set the platter on an end table. Her mouth had a funny slant—not a smile, not a frown.

The look brought a clutch to Vera's stomach. She laid the dress pieces across a chair and hurried to the door in time to see Jacob leading an unfamiliar gray horse into the barn.

A horse wearing Jacob's saddle.

CHAPTER TEN

BEFORE JACOB COULD unsaddle the gray gelding, Vera called his name. He ducked his head and wished for more time to work out his explanation.

Shawl drawn tightly around her, Vera strode into the barn. "Who's this? And where's Curly?"

"I, uh . . ." Jacob focused on unfastening the cinch. "I traded her. This is Flick. Sweet old fella, isn't he?"

"*What?* You traded your prize cutting horse?"

Jacob didn't need reminding what a hard decision he'd made. Actually, it was an easy choice—either trade Curly for sewing machine money or possibly lose Vera forever. Once Jacob explained the situation, Ivan O'Dale had been eager to deal. The man wanted Curly bad enough that he'd gladly upped his offer *and* thrown in Flick as a replacement. The gelding could never match Curly as a cutting horse, but he knew his way around a herd of cattle.

Jacob glanced down to see Vera's toe impatiently tapping the ground. "Answer me."

Lord, give me the words she'll believe. Sliding off Flick's saddle, he pasted on a smile before turning to face Vera. "A neighboring rancher's been hankering after Curly for a long time. He's got a bigger herd to manage and will put her to good use." He forced a light chuckle. "She was getting to be a handful anyway, all full of herself. Flick's a steady ol' boy who'll do just fine for what we need around here."

"I don't believe you, Jacob Collins."

So much for his prayer getting answered.

Vera followed him into the tack room. "I want the truth, and I want it now."

He set the saddle on the rack and started back out with a curry comb, but with Vera blocking the doorway, and looking so pretty doing it even with a scowl on her face, he had no escape. He squared his shoulders. "The truth is, I made a deal with Ivan O'Dale for enough money to . . ." Okay, maybe he wouldn't tell her the *whole* truth yet and spoil his Christmas surprise. "To offset the repair costs on the borrowed sewing machine. You've worked so hard, Vera, and I won't see you taking on any more debt."

Vera's lower lip trembled. She paused only a moment before flinging her arms around Jacob's neck. "Jacob Collins, you are the most amazing man! First you round up a bunch of ladies to help me sew, and then you trade away the horse I never expected you'd ever willingly part with. How can I ever thank you?"

The curry comb had long since fallen to the floor, and Jacob's arms just naturally found their way around Vera's soft curves. He figured he must reek of sweat and dust after all his riding and horse trading, but Vera didn't seem to mind, so he didn't either. "There's one sure way you could thank me," he murmured into the silken curls at her temple. "Say you'll stay in Bryan. Let me take care of you, Vera. Let me love you for the rest of our lives together."

Her hands slid down his chest, and she looked up with a sorrowful smile. "No, Jacob, not until I'm free of my family's debts. I love you too much to encumber you with my problems."

"I don't see it that way. I—" He jerked his chin and swallowed hard. "Wait. Did you just say you love me?"

She gasped as if she had surprised even herself. Then, with a resigned sigh, she leaned against him, her head nestled in the crook of his shoulder. "I do love you. With all my heart, and more than I dreamed possible."

His arms tightened around her. "Then trust me, Vera Mae. Say you'll stay, and I promise everything will be all right."

"Nancy, you look divine." Vera made one small adjustment to the bridal veil. "It's almost time to leave for the church. Shall I call your father in now?"

Giving a nervous nod, Nancy waited while her mother fastened a choker of pearls at her throat, then abruptly caught Vera in a hug. "Thanks to you, I'm going to be the best-dressed lady in Bryan!"

Vera couldn't help the surge of pride rising in her chest. Yes, even Madame Solange Fortier would be impressed with all Vera had accomplished over the past several weeks. Not without help, of course. She'd be eternally grateful to Helen Hicks and her stalwart friends.

And to Jacob. For his help, for his faithfulness . . . for his love.

Opening the bedroom door, she motioned to Ephraim, who paced the hallway. He halted mid-stride, his expression as anxious as Nancy's, and marched over. When he peeked inside the room, he released an admiring sigh.

Vera watched with a twinge of longing as Nancy's parents surrounded her with hugs and good wishes—something Vera herself would miss terribly when her wedding day arrived. She dabbed at an escaping tear and hurried downstairs, where Jacob waited to walk her over to the church.

He looked so handsome in his pressed suit and polished boots. She wished she could have worn something cheerier than the somber gray of her mourning dress. If God allowed, perhaps someday she'd wear white satin and lace to meet her groom at the altar.

She shivered at the thought.

Jacob cast her a concerned glance. "Cold?"

"Perhaps a little."

He tucked her close as they stepped off the Polks' front porch, and she shivered again out of pure delight.

The wedding came off beautifully, and Vera received compliment upon compliment about Nancy's stunning gown. At the reception, Jacob had to fend off more than a few potential clients so Vera could enjoy her cake and punch in peace.

Vera was just grateful to have all the extra sewing behind her so she could look forward to a few unhurried days over Christmas. Much as she'd miss seeing her aunt, uncle, and cousins, after considering the cost of train tickets and the inherent difficulties of winter travel, she had concluded it would be wiser to stay in Texas for the holidays.

And perhaps even longer. Jacob, Miz Georgia, and the ladies in town had almost convinced her how sought after her services would be if she'd consider setting up shop right here in Bryan. Although she suspected Jacob's motives had little to do with fashion design.

One problem remained, though. Until she could afford a sewing machine, business would be extremely slow. And she couldn't buy a sewing machine until she'd cleared her family's debts.

When at last they'd seen the happy couple off to begin their honeymoon, Jacob brought Miz Georgia's buggy around, and the three of them drove back to the ranch. As they pulled up between the house and barn, the sweetest sensation of coming home swept through Vera, and she released an audible sigh.

"What was that for?" Jacob asked.

Miz Georgia laughed softly. "I think I know, but I'll let you figure it out for yourself." She climbed down from the buggy and started toward the porch. "Y'all don't stay out here spoonin' too long. Looks to be a cold night."

Snuggled close to Jacob, Vera didn't feel the cold in the least.

He tilted his head to study her, and a slow smile spread across his lips. "You look happier and more rested than I've seen you in weeks."

"I am. And it's all thanks to you." She nestled her head against his shoulder. "I may still be a long way from settling my family's affairs, but I feel as though I can finally look forward to a hopeful future."

"Isn't that what I've been trying to tell you?" Jacob pulled her more fully into his embrace, and his lips found hers with a kiss that said more than words ever could.

"What do you mean, it's still not here?" Jacob pounded his fist on the counter. "You promised me, Ephraim. It's Christmas Eve."

"I didn't promise anything. I only said it *should* be here by Christmas." Tugging out his pocket watch, Ephraim checked the time. "There's a train due in yet this afternoon. There's still a chance."

"Can't you send another wire, find out what the holdup is?"

"It won't do any good. I'm sorry, Jacob. You'll have to be patient."

Grumbling, Jacob marched to the front window. He stared across the street toward the railroad tracks as if by force of will he could make the train carrying Vera's sewing machine appear.

Absently, he reached into his vest pocket and fingered the small velvet pouch containing his mother's garnet ring. He'd had everything planned out for days—a Christmas proposal, a ring for Vera's finger, and the Singer sewing machine that would make her the most popular seamstress in the county.

Killing time while he waited for the next train due in, Jacob picked up the supplies Miz Georgia had ordered, ate a bite at the diner, and then camped out at the depot with a newspaper. Around two forty-five, a distant rumble and the sound of a train whistle brought him to his feet. Before long, the hulking black engine thundered into town and screeched to a halt alongside the platform.

As the freight cars were offloaded, Jacob eyed each crate in search of any the size of a sewing machine. When he picked out a likely possibility, he hurried over for a closer look. When he spied SINGER SEWING MACHINE COMPANY stenciled across the side, he shouted, "Hallelujah!"

A porter loading the crate onto a dolly shot him a dubious stare. "This is going to Polk's General Store."

"I know! Thank you!" Practically dancing through the streets, Jacob dogged the porter's steps as he wheeled the dolly around to Ephraim's back door. Before the porter could move the crate into the supply room, Jacob had raced to the front to find Ephraim. "It's here! It's here!"

Ephraim excused himself to a customer, then followed Jacob back. To the porter, he said, "No sense unloading it. This man's taking delivery right now." He signed the receipt and handed the porter a coin. Turning to Jacob, he hiked a brow. "There's still the matter of the balance due."

"Got it right here." Jacob pulled an envelope from his inside coat pocket and counted out the bills. "I'll bring the wagon around. Oh, and would you sell me a couple yards of your prettiest red ribbon? Just tell me how much—"

With an understanding chuckle, Ephraim waived his hand. "The ribbon's on me. Merry Christmas, Jacob."

The easy part was getting the crate into the buckboard. The hard part would be keeping Vera from seeing it. He covered it as best he could with a blanket, then tucked supplies in all around.

He could hardly wait for Christmas morning.

CHAPTER ELEVEN

VERA AWOKE TO the aromas of sausage, biscuits and gravy, and Miz Georgia's fresh-brewed coffee. She could hardly wait to see Jacob's face when she gave him his Christmas gift. It would be a special Christmas indeed!

Several of the ranch hands had already gathered in the kitchen by the time Vera had dressed and come downstairs. For this special day, she'd foregone her mourning attire and chosen a deep green gown with an ivory collar. She twisted her hair into a bun, then changed her mind, leaving the curls to flow down her back the way Jacob admired.

"Where's Jacob?" she asked as she helped Miz Georgia carry platters of food to the table.

"Had some chore to finish in the barn. He'll be along shortly."

Jacob bustled in just then, his cheeks pink from the cold and a gleam in his eye that raised goose bumps on Vera's arms. Would he propose today? If he did, Vera had already made up her mind to say yes, because Jacob Collins had taught her how to hope again, and she intended to make the very best of whatever time they had together.

After breakfast, the ranch hands said their thank-yous and returned to their duties, spelling each other for visits with friends or family nearby. Miz Georgia suggested Jacob stoke the fire in the parlor while she and Vera cleaned up the kitchen.

"And take your time," Miz Georgia said with a nod. "We still need to get the turkey in the oven."

"Right." Was that a wink Jacob shot back?

Soon after, Vera wondered what Jacob could be up to in the parlor to make such a racket. Stoking the stove? Sounded more like he'd rearranged all the furniture—twice! She was about to go check on him when the noises ceased and he poked his head in the kitchen.

"Vera Mae," he asked sweetly, "can you come help me a minute?"

"Now? I was about to mix up some stuffing."

A telltale twinkle in her eye, Miz Georgia snatched the spoon from Vera's hand. "The stuffing'll wait. Go see what he needs."

Vera narrowed her eyes at Jacob, but she couldn't suppress a quiver of anticipation. Was this the moment she'd hoped for—a proposal under the Christmas tree? With feigned annoyance, she whipped off her apron before flouncing out of the kitchen. "You've made enough noise in here to—*Oh, Jacob!*"

Next to the tree sat a brand new Singer sewing machine with a big red bow on top. Jacob stood next to it, a mile-wide grin splitting his face. "Merry Christmas, Vera Mae."

"But . . . how?" And then she knew. "Curly. You traded Curly so you could buy this for me." She threw her arms around his neck. "Oh, Jacob, this is the sweetest, most special thing anyone's ever done for me!"

He cradled her cheek, his gaze filled with longing. "Is it enough to convince you to stay?"

"Well . . ." With a demure smile, she lowered her eyes. "It's *almost* enough."

"Don't tease me, Vera Mae." Frustration brought a gravelly roughness to Jacob's voice.

Sorry for prolonging his agony, she laughed softly. "If I stay, it won't be because of a sewing machine. It'll be because of *you*. I love you, Jacob Collins, and I've realized I could never be truly happy anywhere you *aren't*."

His boyish grin returned. "I was hoping you'd come to feel that way. Because there's another gift I'd sure like to give you." Putting some space between them, he took something from his vest pocket before dropping to one knee. "You'll make me the happiest man on earth if you'll accept this ring and say you'll marry me."

A happy sob bubbled up in Vera's throat. She tried to form the word *yes*, but no sound came out and all she could do was nod. Then Miz Georgia's whoop sounded behind her, followed by cheers and clapping outside the parlor windows, where apparently several of the ranch hands had been peeking in and waiting for this moment.

Jacob took her trembling hand and slid a sparkling garnet ring on her finger. Then he rose and enfolded her in his arms, lowering his lips to hers with a kiss that curled her toes. Careless of everyone watching, she kissed him back with abandon.

When finally they broke apart, both breathless and laughing through their tears, Vera remembered the gift she had for Jacob. "I have a surprise for you, too. Wait right here, and I'll call you when it's ready."

Jacob strode from the closed kitchen door to the Christmas tree and back again. Nearly half an hour had passed. What could Vera possibly be doing all this time?

Miz Georgia sidled in but quickly closed the door again. "Don't you be wearing a hole in my floor with all your pacing."

"Is Vera in the kitchen? How much longer?"

"Patience, now. You know a good surprise takes some finagling." With a knowing wink, she toward the sewing machine.

Moments later, the kitchen door opened again. Smile beaming, Vera motioned to Jacob. "It's ready. Come with me."

On their way through, Vera handed Jacob his coat, then wrapped a woolen shawl around her shoulders as she led him outside to the barn. He noticed the ranch hands were still gathered around and watching every move. They all seemed to know something he didn't.

Then he saw it—a big red ribbon tied on the stall that used to be Curly's. A familiar nose poked over the gate, followed by a whinny. In disbelief, Jacob edged closer. There was no mistaking his mare's spiraling forelock. "Curly?" He aimed his wondering gaze at Vera. "How?"

"I knew you'd never willingly part with her, and when you came home that day without her, I had to find out why." Snuggled under Jacob's arm, Vera reached up to stroke Curly's neck. "I paid a visit to Mr. O'Dale one day—"

"You didn't!"

"Don't worry. He never betrayed your confidence. He only said you had some ideas about investing in your future."

Jacob smiled at the truth of those words. "But . . . you bought her back?"

"More of a bartering arrangement." Laughing lightly, Vera rested one hand on Jacob's chest as she gazed up at him. "Did you know Mr. O'Dale has two fashion-conscious daughters, both of whom are getting married in the next several months? I'm about to put *your* Christmas gift to good use."

Before Jacob could think of a single thing to say, Miz Georgia stepped up beside them. "I have a Christmas gift for you, too, Jacob." She handed him a thick brown envelope.

Turning away from the stall, Jacob eyed his boss as he tore open the flap. He unfolded the contents to discover a sheaf of legal papers. "Miz Georgia . . . what is this?"

"It's a contract of sale for the ranch." She held up her hand to keep him from interrupting. "Yes, I've decided it's time for me to retire to that cozy cottage in town."

"But I haven't put aside near enough yet." He tried to give the papers back.

Miz Georgia firmly shook her head. "We'll count your withholdings thus far as the down payment, and I'll hold title while you pay off the rest. But from here on out, consider the ranch yours." A smile on her lips, she took one of his hands and one of Vera's. "Anyway, you'll soon be needing a home for your bride and the passel of young'uns soon to follow."

Vera gasped, but Jacob noticed she wore a surprised smile of her own. Yes, indeed, with all the wedding gowns Vera would be designing, that new Singer sewing machine was about to prove its worth.

Claiming another kiss from his bride-to-be, Jacob decided he couldn't have designed a merrier or more hope-filled Christmas if he'd tried.

HISTORICAL NOTES

The setting for *Designs on Love* is based on historical facts, however. Between 1860 and 1867, the town of Millican, Texas, grew quite prosperous, reportedly the largest Texas city north of Houston and Galveston. Then in 1866 the Houston and Texas Central Railway began expansion to Bryan, and businesses moved north with the railroad. The population of Millican was further reduced by the 1867 yellow fever outbreak. Bryan, in the meantime, was named the new county seat and soon replaced Millican as Brazos County's center of commerce. Today, the metropolitan area of Bryan–College Station boasts over 228,000 residents, while the population of Millican, less than 20 miles away, is only around 250.

ABOUT MYRA JOHNSON

Award-winning author Myra Johnson writes emotionally gripping stories about love, life, and faith. Myra is a two-time finalist for the prestigious ACFW Carol Awards, and her Heartsong Presents romance *Autumn Rains* (November 2009) won RWA's 2005 Golden Heart for Best Inspirational Romance Manuscript. Married since 1972, Myra and her husband are the proud parents of two beautiful daughters who, along with their godly husbands, have huge hearts for ministry. Seven grandchildren take up another big chunk of Myra's heart. Originally from Texas, the Johnsons moved to the Carolinas in 2011. They love the climate and scenery, but they may never get used to the pulled pork Carolinians call "barbecue"! The Johnsons share their home with two very pampered rescue doggies who don't always understand the meaning of "Mom's trying to write."

Find Myra Online

www.myrajohnson.com
www.facebook.com/MyraJohnsonAuthor
Twitter: @MyraJohnson and @TheGrammarQueen
www.amazon.com/author/myrajohnson

Made in the USA
Columbia, SC
19 March 2023

14017844R00059